Marry in Haste

ANNIE SEATON

Richards Brothers: Book 2

Dedication

This book is dedicated to my dear friend, Melissa Lulham, who discovered her own birth grandfather on Lipari Island and inspired Tom and Brianna's story.

Chapter One

The taxi driver tooted his horn and she waved at him to stay. "Five minutes," she called out, her voice shaking. He stepped out of the car and yelled out to her across the rows of headstones.

"Look, love, I don't want to be rude, but if you want to get to the airport in time, we'll have to go now. We're still in morning peak hour and the traffic's heavy."

Brianna Ballantyne's whole life had turned upside down when she'd received the two-page letter from the Italian lawyer three days ago, and her plan to spend twelve months in Australia writing her psychology book flew out the window when she read the typed words she had waited so long to hear.

The letter had led her to her mother's graveside in a small cemetery in Sydney. The grave was unkempt and the long grass brushed against her bare knees. She'd run her fingers over the cold marble and traced the words. Her throat clogged and her eyes pricked with unshed tears.

"Rosa Caranto. b. September 15 1949, Lipari Island – d. March 11 2009, Sydney. A loving daughter."

Her birth mother had died just short of her sixtieth birthday. Brianna had never met her, despite working through an intermediary agency to locate her for more than two years. When they'd notified her they had located her mother, all they would disclose was that she lived in Sydney, Australia. Brianna knew when a person was located they had to give their consent for the applicant to be told their name and to make contact. Her mother had declined, so she had followed the paper trail from Scotland to Australia herself, determined not to give up.

But she had arrived too late. The letter had reached her three days after she'd arrived. It had been forwarded to her Sydney hotel from Scotland, and now she finally knew her mother's name. Instead of giving her the details to contact her mother, the lawyer informed her of her mother's death and the place she was buried. Closing her eyes, she tried to remember where she'd been in March when her mother had passed, but tears filled her eyes and she couldn't think straight.

Damn it all. If only she'd started looking earlier, she might have made it in time and met her. *Why didn't she want me? When I was born and when I found her?*

She brushed away the tears as they wet her cheeks and gripped the piece of paper that had led her to this small beachside cemetery thousands of miles away from her Scottish home. And not only did it tell her about Rosa's death, but about the inheritance of her mother's cottage in Italy and the bizarre conditions attached to it.

She had to be married to get the cottage.

Well, dammit, if that was what it took to find her birth family, she'd bloody well find someone to marry.

"Rosa." She whispered her mother's name as she traced the letters on the small headstone. "What happened to you? Why didn't you didn't want me? Why do you want me to get married?

The horn of the taxi blared again and the driver revved the engine. Still in a daze, Brianna pulled herself to her feet. Looking around, she spotted a clump of white daisies growing wild at the base of a nearby gum tree. She reached down, picked one and walked back to the grave placing it gently beneath the headstone.

"Good-bye, Rosa . . . Mother," she whispered. "I'll be back, one day."

Climbing into the back seat of the taxi, she composed herself before leaning forward. "An extra twenty dollars if you get me there on time." She slipped the letter into the side of her rucksack and fell back in the seat when the driver hit the gas and they sped off towards Sydney International Airport.

Thanks to the strategic, but wild, driving of her taxi driver, she made the airport in time. She unzipped her money belt and handed him a fifty-dollar note when he pulled her suitcase and laptop bag from the trunk and placed them on the curb.

"Thanks, love. Have a good trip." He nodded at her as a waiting passenger opened the front door of the taxi and climbed in. Brianna hitched the computer bag onto her shoulder and turned to pick up her suitcase.

"Oh, no!" Her rucksack was still on the floor of the back of the taxi. She waved madly as the rear of the taxi disappeared around the corner, but it was too late. Thank God her passport and travel documents were in her money belt. She closed her eyes trying to remember what was in her rucksack and groaned when she remembered the letter from the lawyer. She had slipped it into the side pocket when she got back in the taxi.

Hell. She hadn't taken any notice of his details once she'd read the contents. All she knew was his office was on Lipari Island.

Wheeling her suitcase behind her, she decided there was nothing she could do about it now, without missing her check-in. Squaring her shoulders, she moved to the end of the and vowed to be more careful in future.

Ha! As if.

The queue moved slowly and Brianna tapped her foot impatiently as she waited for her turn. No matter how hard she tried, things never came together for her. Her throat clogged. Maybe if she'd been more organised, she might have found her mother somewhere other than her grave? Never mind, she'd survive without the letter. All she had to do was buy a new toothbrush and some underwear, and remember the name of the lawyer once she arrived on Lipari.

Thank goodness, she'd kept her computer out of the rucksack and hadn't lost her manuscript as well. Which reminded her, she'd forgotten to back it up. First job once she was settled on the plane. That was an easy problem to address. Then all she had to do was find someone who was willing to play the part of a loving fiancé.

She had four days to figure that one out.

If only she had more time, she was sure one of her mates from Scotland would have played the part for a holiday in Italy.

Of course . . . that was it! She would pay someone. Surely she would be able find someone to play a role for a couple of days while she checked out the lawyer and Lipari? And found out about this inheritance and the conditions attached. All she wanted was to find out about her mother and why she'd left her thirty years ago. It wouldn't hurt to play act for a few days.

Four days . . . for someone who usually did things at the last minute that would be plenty of time.

Her phone beeped in her pocket and she pulled it out.

"Oh my God." Heads turned and Brianna grinned back as curious looks were directed her way. For once things were going her way. Phil was flying back in to Sydney from Bali and his flight was on time. He was through customs and she'd get to see him before she turned around and flew back to Europe. Now all she had to do was find the coffee shop where he was waiting after she checked in.

Chapter Two

Long, bare legs flashed past the edge of Tomas Richard's vision and he swivelled around as a high-pitched squeal from their owner interrupted his reading of the *Financial Review*. The tall, dark-haired girl slid to a stop on the polished floor of the concourse next to the coffee shop before flinging herself into the waiting arms of a hippy-looking guy with red dreadlocks hanging over his shoulders. His tattooed arms encircled her and she rained kisses on his cheeks, as she wrapped her legs around the hips of the young man.

Tomas was sitting in one of the coffee shops at Sydney International Airport waiting for his flight to Italy to be called. He watched with amusement as the young man disentangled himself and led his girlfriend across to the coffee shop, one arm slung around her shoulder. They stopped in the queue next to Tom's table, and he turned back to the newspaper. The girl's excited chatter drifted across to him.

"I can't believe you got here in time. Oh, Phil, how lucky was it that our flights were on the same day?" Then she clapped her hand over her mouth. "Oh, shit, wait here." She threw her handbag onto the empty table behind Tom's chair, narrowly missing his head, and ran back across to the lounge area. He watched as she retrieved a laptop case from a vacant chair. He shook his head. She was lucky security hadn't removed it. Hadn't she seen the signs everywhere asking passengers not to leave bags unattended? And now she'd left her handbag on the table next to him.

What a scatterbrain.

She placed the laptop case on the table next to her handbag and her hippy boyfriend looped his arm back around her shoulders as they waited to be served.

"What do you mean 'had' a letter?"

Snatches of their conversation rose and fell in the general noise of the café, and Tom tried to concentrate on his newspaper, until the sound of coins hitting the floor interrupted his reading. He lifted his head. Those long tanned legs filled his vision again, and he appreciated the view of a shapely derriere moulded by close fitting cargo shorts when the girl bent to retrieve the scattered coins. As she twisted around, a sapphire blue stone hanging from a ring in her belly button glinted in the light. Her face was level with Tom's and a pair of chocolate-brown eyes stared at him from beneath raised brows. He grinned at her. Okay, so he'd been caught out checking her out. As he returned her bemused look, he realised she was not as young as he'd first thought, so she should doubly appreciate his admiration.

Closer to his age. She should know better than to leave her bags lying around the whole airport. But a nice figure.

He shrugged and turned back to the newspaper as they crossed to the table behind him and their conversation could be heard over the hiss of the coffee machine.

"Well, I sort of left it in the taxi," she said.

"Sort of?" Her boyfriend sounded exasperated and Tom marvelled at his patience. "Brianna, what aren't you telling me?"

"Well, it was in my rucksack and that's still in the taxi, too. But look, it's all good. Now that you're here, you can contact the company and chase it up for me. Much easier than me trying to do it from Italy. Besides, I'm going to be busy. I've got four days to find a husband."

Bloody hell, talk about a soap opera. Tom had heard enough. He folded his newspaper and tucked it under his arm, picked up his laptop, and headed for the boarding gate where he might find more peace and quiet.

The lounge at gate forty-five was deserted and he smiled to himself. Alex, his younger brother had teased him at the country airport this morning because he'd left for Sydney so early. His siblings all liked to rib him about his attention to detail and ticking all the boxes, but it had paid off—little did they know how well, and he wasn't ready to share that news just yet. Excitement filled him at the thought of life on Lipari Island. He had every intention of relaxing and living life to the full. His days of working in an office were over—careful planning and wise investments had enabled him to do that. He'd only bought the marina to help Aunt Carmen out.

Tom waited for his flight to be called as the early afternoon queue of departing international flights started on the runway. His other brother, Nick, had been the only fly in the ointment when he'd questioned his decision to take off for Italy. Nick had called the shots for too many years. He had married life, and Lissy, to focus on now. His years of wandering the Pacific were over, and if Tom wanted to head to Italy and become the brother with the wanderlust, it was none of Nick's damn business. It had taken him a few months to wrap up his contract at the university and sell his apartment. He didn't want to leave any loose ends behind him. Now Nick and Lissy had been married for eight months, and Alex and Emily were engaged. Tom shook his head; Alex was barely out of university and way too young to think about getting married. But despite both his brothers having partners, Tom was content sitting here alone. Women were trouble.

He did hope his two brothers had chosen

wisely. As for him, he'd pulled his office door shut for the last time on Friday afternoon and closed a chapter in his life without a backward glance. For the first time in a long while, he was looking forward to the coming weeks.

Tom folded his newspaper and waited for his flight to be called.

***

The 'now boarding' sign flashed next to the Sydney to Rome flight on the departure board, and Brianna hugged Phil. It had taken ages to calm him down after she had dropped the bit about finding a husband.

"It was great to catch up. I'm sorry I have to go so soon." She blinked back the tears that seemed to be ever present since she'd received the letter from the lawyer.

Phil pushed her back, placed his hands on her shoulders, and bent down to look into her face. "I'm worried about you. Forget this stupid idea, no matter what the letter says. Take some time to find out what it's all about."

"That's what I haven't got. I've only to the end of the week to turn up or the cottage goes to someone else. The blasted letter has followed me around the world." She took a deep breath and tried to make him understand. "This is my last opportunity to find out about my birth mother, Rosa. I have the chance to live where she lived, to talk to people who knew her. I'll do anything it takes to grab that chance with both hands."

"No, they wouldn't care. I haven't even told them I found her or about the inheritance, so please keep it to yourself." She sighed and pulled her braid across her shoulder. "You know what Mum can be like."

"You're too hard on her, Brianna." Phil pulled her close for a brotherly hug and she rested her head on his shoulder. "Even though she doesn't show it, she loves you. She's just a very private person. Anyway, at least you're on leave from work. You can live anywhere and write your book. Promise me you won't do anything stupid."

Brianna smiled back at him. Phil had looked out for her since his parents had adopted her as a baby, and she'd always respected him as a sensible, older brother. She'd never fitted in with the family, her adoptive parents were staid and elderly now, and couldn't understand her desire to travel the world when she had a secure job at home in Scotland. Reaching over, Brianna tugged Phil's long dreadlocks. He had the complexion and hair colouring of a true Scotsman, even though he looked more like a hippy with his wild hair and patterned pants. Their parents accepted Phil travelling the world, so why did she always feel like the outsider in the family?

"I think Dad would be more upset about

your hair than me taking off to the wilds of some Italian island. It's okay, chill. Once I see the lawyer, I'll get all the details and I'll email you."

The robotic voice of the announcer came across the system. "Final call for Qantas flight QF46 to Rome. Calling passenger Brianna Ballantyne. The gate is about to close. Please make your way to the boarding gate immediately."

"Oh, damn . . . how embarrassing." She grabbed her bags and leaned over and kissed Phil's cheek before she headed toward the security corridor. "If you're talking to Mum and Dad, you can tell them you saw me and I'm fine."

Phil gave her a wave and she strode along the corridor. Luckily, the checkpoint queue had cleared.

Jeez, I can't believe I've only been in Australia for five days and now I've got that god-awful twenty-hour flight back to Europe again.

It would have been a shorter flight if she'd gone through Dubai, but she'd pick up a good deal online through Qantas. Two international flights in over a week had severely dented the advance payment she'd received for her book.

She quickly cleared security through to the duty free area and then realised gate forty-five was at the far end of the terminal. "Oh, damn, that's all I need! Miss the flight. Get your skates on, girl," she said to herself running for the gate. Grateful for her flat boots, she sprinted along the concourse and ignored the accelerated walking bays. Arriving at the gate with seconds to spare, she pulled out her boarding pass and hurried down the jet bridge. The cabin services officer smiled and he directed her to the row at the back of the plane, before he turned and pulled the door down. Most of the passengers were already settled into their allocated seats and belted in.

"Excuse me. Oh, sorry." She pushed past the few passengers who remained standing and were loading their luggage into the overhead compartments. Her laptop bumped the seats all the way up the aisle and she apologised, hitching it higher on her shoulder. She cursed softly when she reached her seat at the very back of the plane and opened the hatch above her seat row to find it was already crammed full with bags.

I hate it when that happens. Next time I'll be on time, she promised herself.

She handed her laptop over to one of the cabin staff to stow it in another compartment. Glancing down at her boarding pass, she smiled when she saw she'd been allocated the window seat. No matter how many times she flew, she preferred sitting near the window so she could see the ground approach when the plane landed on *terra firma*.

"Excuse me." She smiled at the man sitting in the middle of the three-seated row. The aisle seat was vacant. "I need to get past."

He ignored her.

"Excuse me." She stood with her hands on her hips as the fasten seatbelt sign came on and the steward gestured for her to be seated. She shrugged her shoulders and pointed to the man who was ignoring her, and then she realised he had earbuds in. She reached out and tapped his shoulder, and when he looked up, she grinned at him. It was the sleaze who'd been checking her out in the coffee shop.

"Sorry," she said pointing to the window. "I'm in the window seat. I need to get through." He closed the laptop and slid his legs to the side so she could get past. Settling into her seat, she reached over and held out her hand.

"I'm Brianna. I hate flying and I talk too much when I'm nervous so I'll apologise in advance."

He ignored her outstretched hand and nodded at her briefly before turning back to the computer screen. She'd had a brief glimpse of deep blue eyes beneath lowered lids set in a tanned face. He was a big man, tall and broad, and he looked uncomfortable in the small airline seat.

He is a bit of a sort though.. Might as well have something decent to look at during the flight, even if he is going to ignore me.

"Pleasure to meet you too, mister. Wake me

up when we get to Singapore," she said. But the sarcasm was wasted as the earbuds remained in his ears and his gaze fixed on the screen. With a yawn, she settled into her seat and closed her eyes, but sleep eluded her as she wondered how the hell she was going to find the lawyer, find a fiancé and claim her inheritance.

Four days to find a husband. The mantra echoed through Brianna's head.

Chapter Three

After the jet reached cruising altitude, the seat belt sign went off. Tom looked across at the woman sleeping beside him. She was sprawled like an adolescent stretched out on a sofa. Her long bare legs finished in short socks and boots, and took up the space in front of his seat. He undid his lap belt and moved one seat across to the vacant seat next to the aisle, so they both had a bit more space.

When she'd shoved past him to the seat, he'd been scrutinised by a piercing gaze, and a shiver had snaked down his spine. He was surprised by the strong Scottish accent. He hadn't noticed that in the airport. He'd pegged her for an Aussie or Italian with her olive skin. Her parting shot about being a pleasure to meet him had him smothering a grin. She might be a scatterbrain, but she was feisty.

And quite beautiful.

Even in repose, her eyes were circled by dark shadows. Soft pink lips were parted as she slept beside him, breathing softly. Her olive skin was unblemished, and dark lashes fanned onto high cheekbones. A long plaited braid lay across her chest, which rose and fell with each breath. He wondered where she was going and why she looked so exhausted. Before she'd fallen asleep, he'd noticed her dab at her eyes a couple of times. He'd shrugged and turned his laptop on.

Not my problem. He had no idea why she was so desperate to find a husband and he didn't want to know. He'd had enough of women to last him a lifetime, although when he looked at Lissy and Nick, he knew they were perfect for each other. God knows he needed a change after the fiasco with Jill. He'd been sucked in by her and she'd played right along, always interested in the plan he'd mapped out for his life.

And too interested in his financial status he'd discovered just in time.

Her parting shot about his boring corporate life when she told him about the husband she'd left behind in Melbourne, had cemented his desire to get away. He'd called Italy and finalised the paperwork with his aunt's lawyer the same day.

He was well aware he held the reputation of being the boring brother, but he preferred to think of himself as sensible. His shrewd and careful approach to playing the stock market through the global financial crisis had paid off, and he'd made a killing, although only his broker knew how successful he'd been. It had given him the opportunity to dump his career and buy the marina. He'd never have to work again if that's what he decided he wanted out of life. He would stay commitment free and that was the way he wanted it.

Closing his eyes, he thought about the next

few months. He had to find somewhere to live. He knew how small his aunt's apartment was, and besides, he preferred to live alone. Then he'd sort out the finances of the marina and get a handle on the day-to-day running of the tourist side of things. He'd exchanged several emails with Aunt Carmen's accountant and it looked like he would be able to leave that side of things as they were. Then it was time to start living and experience life beyond the four walls of an office—he was way overdue for a bit of fun. He smiled to himself. By about ten years. Everything a man could ask for in his life—great career, secure finances, and solid investments—had come to him through dedication and hard work. But restlessness had overtaken him over the months since Nick's wedding. What was he missing out on?

He opened up his laptop and tapped away at the keyboard, and began a list. To pass the time, he thought of some ludicrous things that were totally out of character and added them.

Didn't hurt to dream.

"How many guys do you know who wear a suit on a holiday to Europe?" Alex, his youngest brother had teased him at the airport when they saw him off to Sydney.

He'd pushed Alex's hand away as he'd played at straightening Tom's tie. "One of the sons in this family has to dress respectably. However, I'm not going to have a haircut while I'm away, and the suit will go in the cupboard as soon as I unpack."

"I'll believe it when you email me a photo." Alex had laughed.

Now Tom grinned to himself as he typed 'get a tattoo' and then deleted it and typed 'get an earring.' That would send a message to everyone who thought he was a bore. Staid old Tom with an earring and long hair?

Stuff it, he'd do it. After all, who knew him on the island? He grinned as he imagined a whole new persona for himself, focused on having a good time. He looked forward to sending a photo to his brothers. Ten minutes later, a definitive list of ten things he intended to achieve in Italy filled his screen.

"Can I make a suggestion?" A quiet voice close to his ear startled him. He looked across and was taken aback to see his seat neighbour was awake and reading the list on his screen.

"And that would be?"

"Sounds like you're planning a great trip," she said with one eyebrow raised and her head to the side. "Jet ski . . . ride a bike, and—"

"Didn't anyone ever tell you it's rude to read over someone's shoulder?"

A wide grin spread across her face and she nodded. "Yes, but you were so focused on your typing, I was curious. Sounds like a good holiday," she said without a hint of apology.

"Yes, I do plan on having a good holiday," he finally said. "Anyway, what was your suggestion?" It would be too rude to totally ignore her. He'd already done that once and heard her smart-mouthed comment.

"Depends on what sort of motorbike you're going to ride. The Italian Grand Prix is on in Mugello next month. I've heard it's worth seeing if you love your motorbikes, but if you want tickets, you'll need to book them well in advance."

Tom stared at her. "No, I'm not into motorbikes. I'm going to get myself a pushbike."

"Wow, you are a thrill seeker." She put her hand over her mouth to cover a giggle. "And here was I thinking you were a bit of a balloon."

"A balloon?"

Her face was full of mirth and she held his gaze as her lips twitched. *What the hell was she on about?* Just his luck to sit next to someone who was two bricks short of a load.

"Sorry, I keep forgetting I'm not in Scotland. A balloon…" She tipped her head to the side and he read the mirth in her expression. "Ah . . . it's someone who thinks they are pretty damn good. After all, I did catch you checking out my wee arse." When he looked at her blankly, she leaned forward and pointed behind her. Her bare leg pressed against his thigh as she twisted in the seat.

"My backside!"

"Oh." He wasn't quite sure if she was complaining or teasing him, and for a fleeting moment he was tempted to make a smart reply about her butt. But her Scottish burr made it impossible to read her tone, and he didn't want to offend her. He moved away from the warmth of her leg, which was still connecting with his. She straightened and settled back in her seat. Her chin was propped in her hand on the divider between them as she continued to read the list over his shoulder.

"What were you going to add to my list?"

"I don't know you, so I hope you won't be offended." She unclipped her belt, flipped back the arm of the seat, and slid across to the middle seat so she could get a better look at his screen.

"You have my interest," he said waiting as the warmth of her bare shoulder pressed into his shirt. She concentrated for a moment, and he watched as her gaze flicked down his typed list before she placed her hand over her mouth and covered a giggle. "I'm sorry." She snorted and then burst out laughing. "I can't believe you've written a list. I don't think I've ever written one in my life. So my suggestion would be to stop writing lists and start doing some of it!"

Tom leaned over and typed # 11 . . . stop making lists. He looked over at the woman sitting next to him who was watching him closely. Her deep brown eyes were fringed by thick dark lashes and her expression still brimmed with mirth. The shadows around her eyes had faded a little after her nap. They had been in the air for four hours and she'd slept soundly the whole time.

"I hope I haven't insulted you. I'm pretty good at doing that, or so my family tells me," she said. "They say I should learn to think before I open my mouth."

Tom snapped his laptop shut and leaned forward to put it in the carry bag. He bumped his head on the back of the seat in front of him and had to bend sideways to retrieve the bag.

Christ, they made these seats for midgets, not six foot plus tall men.

He turned his attention back to Brianna when the laptop was safely stowed.

"No. No offense taken. Not at all. Maybe, as you suggest, I do need to lighten up a bit." He looked back at her. "After all…it's on the list."

"Well, I'm the person to do it. And you have the pleasure of my company for another sixteen hours unless you are only going to Singapore?"

"No, I'm going all the way through to Rome." He surprised himself sharing information with a chance-met stranger. She loosened his tongue with her constant questions and he'd quite enjoyed her banter about his list making. "I'm going to Italy mainly for business."

"So, let's try again," she said with a smile and held out her hand. "I'm Brianna."

"Tomas." He took her hand and held it a little longer than he normally would have, as unexpected warmth shot up his arm.

"So are you a businessman or holidaying?" Brianna pulled her hand out of his and reached over and touched his narrow navy-blue tie. "The suit and the computer. I had you picked for a business traveller when I saw you in the coffee shop. In fact, I'm surprised to see you slumming it back here in economy. You looked like you should be up front in business, not in cattle class."

"Waste of money. Why pay thousands of dollars extra for a seat to get to the same destination for a glass or two of champagne."

"Ah. I bet you work in finance."

Another woman on the make. That's the last thing he needed next to him for eighteen hours. It was time to pull back and stop acting like the "right balloon" she had pegged him as. He gave her a non-committal nod. "And I have some work I must finish."

He'd just put the laptop away, so he pulled out the newspaper he'd already read from back to front out of the seat pocket. He wasn't worried about hurting the feelings of someone he'd never see again, and glanced across at her as he opened the newspaper and was surprised to see a huge grin plastered on her face. Her opinion of him was written in her expression.

"Okay, I'll leave you in peace and stop the twenty questions."

She slid back to the window seat and placed the headphones over her ears and reached forward to fiddle with the control of the small viewing screen on the back of the seat in front of her. Even though he'd ended the conversation, Tom decided he had been dismissed. He leaned back in his seat and closed his eyes. This was going to be a long flight . . . maybe he should have spent the extra and flown business class. He could afford it, but old habits died hard.

***

The voice of the captain announcing they were commencing the descent into Singapore roused Brianna from a deep sleep. She rubbed her eyes with the backs of her hands and pulled the earphones out. They'd slipped across her face and were now snagged in her hair.

"Damn," she said softly. Tugging at them only made it worse. She tried to untangle the hair caught around the posts, but they snagged even more tightly. Glancing over at Tom, she was pleased to see he was awake and typing on the keyboard.

"Could I have some help here, please?"

Tom looked up from his screen and then closed the lid and slipped the computer into the seat pocket in front of him. He moved closer and lifted her hands away from the tangled hair and cable, and placed them in her lap.

"You let go, I'll do it. You certainly have it tangled."

"Ow," she cried. He unwound a strand of dark hair from the cable on the earphones and she closed her eyes.

"Sorry, I'll try to be gentle. Relax."

Brianna leaned forward, and warm, gentle fingers brushed against her cheek. His hands smelled like citrus, and she smiled to herself as he tried to untangle the cord from her hair. She'd noticed his manicured nails when he was typing his list earlier.

"Move closer."

She dropped her head lower and leaned across into his shoulder to help him. Peering down, she had a clear view of taut thighs encased in trousers with sharp creases and a pair of polished shoes, and a frisson of attraction skipped her heart rate up a notch.

"There you go."

She sighed with relief when he handed her the earphones. After putting them back in the seat pocket, she ran her fingers through the loosened hair and tried to wind it back into her braid.

"Thank you so much." She looked up and smiled at him." For a while there, I was thinking I would be leaving the plane with them stuck in my hair. I'm overdue for a trim."

She'd planned to get her hair cut in Sydney, but the letter and the rush to change her travel arrangements and book the flight to Rome had interfered with *all* her plans. Not that planning was one of her strengths. She'd been lucky the travel agent had been able to book her all the way to Lipari with ease. All she had to do now was not lose her itinerary. Luckily the Burrough Medical Service back home in Edinburgh had given her a year's leave to finish her book, and she'd planned to stay in Australia for at least half of that. The deadline from the publisher was creeping closer every day and she'd started to panic. Most of her advance had been spent on travel, so she had to make the deadline. She'd need the rest of the money to sort out her current problem.

Hopefully this cottage on Lipari would have somewhere she could sit and write, and get her first draft finished and back to the publisher. Tears pricked her eyes as she thought of that lonely unkempt grave back in Sydney. She'd managed not to think about it since she'd woken from her nap, and she sighed as the grief filled her chest. Brushing the tears away with the back of her hand, she glanced up and saw Tomas watching her. "Sorry, I was miles away. Did you say something?"

"Only that it would be a shame to cut your hair. It's beautiful."

"Are you hitting on me?" As soon as the words left her mouth, she regretted them.

"Certainly not." His voice was frosty and he stared at her. "I don't need to hit on women."

She looked at him as he lounged back in the seat. His dark hair deepened his tanned skin and his cold gaze was fixed on her. An observer may have been fooled by the relaxed and casual position, but there was nothing casual in his unswerving observation of her. A flicker of discomfort shimmied down her spine.

"No matter. I won't be insulted." She forced her lips into an apologetic smile. "Sorry, Tom . . . is it okay if I call you Tom? Look, I was teasing. I grew up in a family with a brothers and lots of male cousins, and I protected myself through childhood by tormenting them before they could get at me. I guess it comes naturally, and I usually lead with my mouth and then my brain kicks into gear." She placed her hand on his arm and then pulled it back when he dropped his gaze down to it. His mouth was set in a cold, straight line.

"Look, I didn't mean to insult you. If someone wants to hit on me, that's flattering, but I expect honesty. And like I told you before, I always babble on too much. So if you want some peace and

quiet on the next leg you can always change seats."
She pointed to the vacant seat across the aisle.

"There's no need for that," he said.
"Besides, we've landed. We're in Singapore"

The wheels bounced onto the tarmac and she
glanced out of the window to see the puff of smoke
as the rubber hit the ground. Relief coursed through
her body and all thoughts of Rosa, the inheritance,
and her deadlines flew from her mind.

"Oh wow, we've landed! And I didn't even
have to worry. I hate landing . . . it's not the flying.
I usually put the music on and close my eyes and
ignore it, but you took my mind off it. Thanks so
much." She looked up and caught a bemused look
on his face. "Woops, I'm prattling on again, aren't
I? I told you I talk too much. If you get sick of me
babbling, tell me to put a sock in it."

A slow smile spread across Tom's face and
she grinned up at him when he shook his head at
her. Relief coursed through her. That was one less
thing she had to worry about.

"Look, I'm sorry for being a pain. It's been
a big week. I'm sure you'll keep me entertained and
the rest of the flight will pass very quickly."

"How about you buy me a cup of tea to
apologise for being rude? I'm sure we can get a
decent cup in the airport somewhere." She smiled
up at him and although the daunting stare had
disappeared, she sensed his reluctance. "Don't

worry, no strings attached."

"Sounds like a plan."

Leaning forward, she checked her money belt was secure and tightened it around her waist. She was not going to lose anything else, especially while they were in Singapore. They disembarked and strolled through the retail area of the airport, and Brianna looked around in appreciation at the huge gardens down the centre of the concourse. Tropical orchids of every imaginable colour cascaded in garlands from lush foliage and the perfume overlaid the usual sterile, artificial smell of most airports. As they walked on, a large display of tropical and temperate orchids hung into a pond filled with bright orange, red, and yellow koi.

"How amazing is that?" she exclaimed. "That's one thing I'm looking forward to in Italy— the gardens. Are you a gardener, Tom?"

He gave her a reluctant smile. "No, I live in an apartment and any plant I ever had died from neglect."

"Well, that's another thing for your list." She tipped her head to the side and wrinkled her nose at him. "No, scrub that. Not exciting enough. You can have a garden when you're old." She grabbed his arm and dragged him into the Starbucks at the edge of the orchid garden and slid onto the padded bench seat along the wall. "I hope Starbucks is up to your coffee tastes."

"Starbucks in Singapore. Hmm . . . we'll see. Okay, I'm buying. How do you like your coffee?" he asked.

"Tea, please," she said and leaned back against the soft padded back of the seat. She was stiff and sore and they'd only travelled for eight hours. The second leg of the flight was another twelve hours and her body was telling her she'd spent too much time in planes in the last week.

Tom stood at the end of the long queue at the counter. Even as he waited in the crowd, his bearing showed what her adopted mother referred to as "good breeding." When he stepped forward to be served, she had a clear view of him, and Brianna smiled to herself. He was tall and broad shouldered, and held himself straight. His eyes were bright and his cheeks had the fresh glow of good health, of someone who looked after himself. Her gaze travelled down from his wide shoulders to his broad chest and his snug-fitting white business shirt. He'd shed the jacket on the jet bridge as the humidity had hit them and rolled his sleeves up to his elbows. Long legs ended in a nice butt. Even in the suit pants. She looked up and caught his cool glance before he turned back to the counter. The heat rose in her cheeks.

He might be a looker, but he needs to lighten up.

She wasn't going to let him get away with

the cool responses and grinned at him when he placed a tray loaded with a variety of food on the table. She'd get a laugh out of him if it took the whole damn trip.

What's good for the goose is good for the gander. "Sprung. We're even now."

He raised his eyebrows without speaking, but it was clear he understood what she was referring to.

"Okay, thanks. I owe you a meal, or several meals by the look of this," she said. He sat and reached for his coffee and leaned back, silently watching the hustle and bustle of Changi airport go past them as Brianna demolished most of the food.

"I won't need to eat again till Italy." She smothered a burp and giggled. "Oops. Sorry . . . bad manners. My mother would be horrified."

He looked across at her and she held his gaze. Even though he didn't smile much, when he did, the crinkly smile lines around his deep blue eyes softened his angular face. Even though she'd only met him eight hours ago, she still felt comfortable with him and sensed his grumpiness was a bit of a shield.

She tipped her head to the side and tapped her finger on her chin.

"Tell me a little about you, Tom. Where's home for you? Do you live in the city or are you from the outback?"

"No, certainly not the outback. I grew up in small rural city, Armidale. It's inland from the north coast. I went to Sydney to university and then back to the country after I graduated." He looked at her. "What about you? How long were you in Australia?"

"Ach, my wee accent has given me away as a tourist, then?" she said, exaggerating her Scottish lilt.

"Just a little."

Finally she'd got another smile out of him

"Well, I'd only been in Australia a few days when I received—" She hesitated. Even though she could babble on like a brook, she was circumspect about giving personal details to strangers. And he was a stranger. For all she knew, he could be setting her up. Her family always told her she trusted too easily and wore her heart on her sleeve. "I received some sudden family news that meant an unexpected trip to Italy. Good news. So no, I have no idea where your city is. I visited Sydney and that was it."

"What about your boyfriend? Weren't you travelling together?"

"My boyfriend?"

"The guy at the airport . . . with . . . er . . . with the hair."

"God, no. Phil's my brother. He's been over here for six months and he'd just flown back in from Bali. It was an absolute coincidence we were

33

at the airport at the same time. We were going to travel around Australia together for a few months. No boyfriends or husbands in my life. I'm a career woman through and through."

She looked down at her khaki shorts and T-shirt. "Even though I look like a tourist, I do have some work to do, and I was going to settle at my sister's place after a wee trip around."

"What sort of work?"

"Oh, a bit of work I can do anywhere. Now we were talking about you. Tell me why you're going to Italy seeing as you're not the big financial businessman who travels in business class." She sensed his hesitation and was interested to see if he would answer her question.

"I'm going over to help my aunt. My uncle died a few months ago and she has a business to run. I am going to help out for a while. See a bit of the country and have a bit of a holiday."

"What do you do? No, don't tell me, let me think about it and then we'll play twenty questions on the plane to pass the time." She looked down at her watch and slumped her shoulders. "Jeez, after all we've got another twelve more hours to fill in."

***

Brianna shifted in the window seat and leaned her head against the recess around the window. It was pitch dark outside and the only thing to look at was the light flashing on the end of the wing. Tom sat up in his aisle seat, his back straight and his arms crossed in front of him. He looked down at the vacant seat between them. Somehow Brianna had managed to fill it with magazines, food wrappers, and a calico money belt. He reached over and rescued her passport, which was about to slip out of the belt onto the floor, and handed it to her.

"You might need this," he said.

She tipped her head to the side and looked back at him for a long moment before speaking, her expression serious for once and he took the opportunity to study her deep brown eyes. They were flecked with gold and her eyelashes were dark and lush, and he was sure it was all natural. She wore no other makeup. A sudden shaft of desire shot through him and he held her gaze. His eyes travelled down her face to her throat and to the soft swell of her breasts beneath her snug T-shirt. Brianna was the first to look away and bent down and slipped her passport back into the belt before leaning forward and slipping it over her head

"Thanks, the belt was sticking into me and kept me awake. That's the last thing I need to lose, isn't it?"

"Yes, you will need your passport."

"I'm hopeless. Always seem to lose things," she said before pushing her long legs out as far as she could to reach her arms above her head and held the back of the seat. "My family has given up on me. They know not to buy me anything expensive because I always lose it."

Tom lifted his gaze from the T-shirt stretched tight against her small firm breasts.

He changed the subject. "Sounds like you come from a big family? Happy childhood?"

"Happy enough." Her voice was a little sad.

"Brothers and sisters?"

"One sister and one brothers, both married, and a tribe of nephews and nieces."

Brianna put her head to the side and tapped her finger on her cheek, moving his attention from her family. "Now, my turn. Let me guess what you do. You said you went to university?"

He nodded.

"A lawyer?"

This time, Tom shook his head.

"Shame. Okay, your turn."

***

Three hours later, a light meal had been served and cleared, and now the cabin was dim again. The movement in the plane had slowed as passengers slept and the cabin staff came through with the occasional offer of water. Tom's body clock was out of sync and he was wide awake.

Neither he nor Brianna had been able to guess the other's profession, and they had exhausted their twenty questions. Tom wouldn't budge and was enjoying the frustration he could see building in Brianna as she ticked off careers.

She was getting ridiculous now and was whispering her way through the alphabet. When she got to zookeeper and he shook his head, she turned to him and took his face between her hands. Her fingers were warm against his skin, and he resisted the temptation to reach up and hold them there. "I've been guessing for three hours now and I am not going to be able to get to sleep until I know. So you tell me and I'll tell you. Deal?"

"Deal, you go first."

"No, you go first."

"You go first... okay... rock, paper, scissors..."

Brianna raised her eyebrows as they put out their fists and fingers and Tom lost.

"Well, come on...spill."

"I am—" he paused for a moment "—a bursar."

"I knew it, I knew it," she squealed and then looked around at the other passengers sleeping and put her hand over her mouth. "I was right then when I guessed accountant." She put on a mock pout. "You didn't play fair. I guessed that straight after lawyer."

"Okay," Tom said. "I'm sorry, but it wasn't exactly what I do. A bursar is a financial administrator. I guess the difference is I don't play with numbers anymore, I manage the staff. Now it's your turn." He was very interested to hear what she did. "I've exhausted every possible profession—" He widened his eyes in mock horror "—barring the oldest profession in the world."

She made him wait for a full minute before she answered. "I've taken twelve months' leave from my job."

He tipped his head to the side waiting for her to continue. "And?"

"I'm a clinical psychologist. I work mainly with couples with relationship problems."

Tom was cross with himself. That'd be right. Of all people to get chatty with, he had to pick a psychologist. He thought back over their conversation—he'd not mentioned anything private that he could remember. He didn't have relationship problems, just preferred to keep his life private and not share his feelings with anyone. So much for the free-spirited Scottish lass he'd thought was interested in his family.

He picked up his sunglasses and fitted the headphones into his ears. She could go and find someone else to psychoanalyse. "I think I'll sleep for the rest of the flight. Good night, Brianna."

Chapter Four

"Pompous jerk," thought Brianna. She'd sat there stewing over his reaction for the three hours he'd slept, or pretended to sleep, because he'd fidgeted the whole time and she knew he was awake and was avoiding talking to her. Unable to sleep, she was now cross and tired and she let her thoughts go back to her mother's grave in Sydney. Instead of wasting time exchanging pleasantries with Tomas, she should have been planning how she was going to sort out her problems when she got to the island.

"Just water, please." Tom smiled at the steward as he poured chilled water into a cup and placed it onto the tray in front of him.

Brianna took a sip of her red wine and looked out the window. She was so angry he'd turned from her when she had revealed her profession. She'd had a glass of wine hoping it would put her to sleep, but it had the opposite reaction and now the thoughts were scurrying around in her head again. Her throat tightened and she gripped the wine glass as she stared into the dark. According to the flight screen on the back of the seat, they were flying over the Himalayas, but it was pitch dark outside.

Bloody stuffed shirt. She settled down into

her seat and sipped on her wine determined to ignore him. God, if she told him her book was about sex therapy he'd probably have a conniption and request another seat. The disappointing thing was that she'd thought they'd hit it off. For someone in her profession, she was such a lousy judge of character. She'd been enjoying their playful conversation and the flight had passed quickly. As soon as he found out she was a psychologist, he'd turned away from her and pretended to sleep. At least she'd managed to forget about her mother and the inheritance and all the other problems looming in front of her. Thank God she hadn't prattled on about that. One thing to be grateful for, at least.

She glanced at her watch and did the time conversion. They were still four hours from Rome. She put her wine glass on the tray and tucked the pillow under her head, determined to get some sleep. It seemed like minutes later and she woke as the captain's voice came over the announcement system. "Ladies and gentlemen, we are making our final approach to Rome."

Her eyes flew open and she sat up straight in her seat, clenching her fingers together in her lap. "Oh, shit, I've left it too late. Inhale, exhale. Simplicity of breath. Inhale, exhale," she muttered under her breath. She closed her eyes again, ready to meditate her way through her fear and ignore the actual landing.

Inner peace and enlightenment. Breathe. Inhale. Exhale. Breathe. Inhale. Exhale.

A tentative hand tapped on her shoulder and she opened her eyes. Tom's nose was about an inch away from hers.

"Are you all right?" He was frowning and those blue eyes were full of concern.

"No, I'm not bloody all right. We're about to land."

"Oh, that's all right then. I thought you were still angry with me."

Brianna turned to him as the anger burned back up from her stomach. He might have taken the time to get to know her a little bit on this flight, he might have seen her with Phil in carefree mode, and he might have played word games with her, but this uptight *eejit* had no idea about her temper.

Tipping her head to one side, she allowed a sweet smile to cross her face and unclenched her fingers and placed her hand on his arm. She gripped it and allowed her nails to bite into his skin.

"Cross with you? Now why would I be cross with a perfect human being like you? Tom, I'm so glad I met you on this flight. I will strive to be like you for the rest of my days. And I will also start making a list so that I don't upset stuffy guys who sit next to me and think I am psycho-analysing them when I'm just trying to be friendly." She waited for him to turn away and ignore her.

I've overdone it this time, but by God, I am so sick of being judged.

All her life, she'd tried to be the daughter, her adopted mother, Jennifer, had expected her to be. She'd failed miserably. The hope of meeting her birth mother had finally died in a lonely cemetery and the events of the last few days had overwhelmed her. This poor guy had been the one to wear her temper. Before she could apologise, Tom reached into the seat pocket and pulled out his computer. His face was without expression and he didn't speak.

Shit, I've pushed his buttons too much this time. The sooner I get off this plane the better.

Tom tapped away at the keys for a few seconds and turned the screen to face her so she could read it. He had added number twelve to his list. She read it and she shook her head and smiled at him.

#12   Don't insult beautiful clinical psychologists on planes. Sorry for being such a jerk.

A row of little smiley emoticons was at the end of the typed words.

Brianna burst out laughing. "Put the computer away. The seat belt sign just came on."

The intercom crackled and the captain's voice announced the imminent landing. "Cabin crew, prepare for descent."

Tom closed his computer and slid it into the

seat pocket before reaching over and taking her hand. "I really am sorry. Apology accepted?"

"Okay. I'm sorry, too." She squeezed his hand, grateful for the comfort he was giving her. "I've had a pretty emotional week and you wore it. And I was nervous about the landing."

Tom smiled and pointed out the window. "*Benvenuti all' Aeroporto Internazionale Leonardo da Vinci di Fiumicin*," he said in perfect Italian

She looked out the window just as the wheels hit the tarmac.

"Hey, two landings and I missed both of them." She looked down at his hand, which was squeezing hers back. "Thanks to you. And I'll take back that stuffy guy comment. You're forgiven."

Brianna was amazed at his perfect Italian, or it had sounded perfect to her. "Where did you learn to speak such perfect Italian?" She turned and looked earnestly at him. "And I am interested as a friend. I'm not in psychoanalysis mode."

"My mother was born on Lipari Island . . . it's off Sicily. That's where my aunt still lives. She was already married when their parents emigrated to Australia, so she stayed there. She's a lot older than my mother, and now she's widowed. She needed some help, so I volunteered." He laughed and shook his head. "I might add, to the great amazement of my entire family. You picked me well. I am a boring balloon. So to answer your

43

original question, we all learned to speak Italian at our mother's knee. She wanted us to speak both languages."

"No shit! That is amazing." She put her hand over her mouth. "Oh, I don't mean amazing you speak Italian. I mean . . . it's amazing you're going to Lipari." She ran her hand through her loose hair." "So am I . . .I mean . . .Lipari Island. That's where I'm going too."

Tom smiled at her. "Are you catching the ferry across from Naples?"

"Yes, I'm catching the train to Naples tomorrow and then getting the midday ferry across on Tuesday."

Lipari Island was a very small place. She'd looked it up on Google Earth. It would be great to know someone there who could speak Italian because she had a feeling the inheritance situation may become a little messy, and if she was honest, she was pleased she wouldn't be saying goodbye to Tom when they got off the plane. "What about you?"

"I'm flying to Naples tonight and then catching the Tuesday ferry. Looks like we'll catch up then. Where are you staying in Naples?"

Oh. My. God. Brianna stared at him and let her mouth drop open as a crazy idea hit her. She shut it and covered it with her hand as she stared at him.

Maybe . . . just maybe . . . the answer to her problem had been sitting next to her all the way to Italy. An over six foot perfectly believable answer who should be able to convince anyone he was her husband-to-be. All she had to do was get him to agree to it. Thoughts scurried around in her head.

"Brianna?" He looked at her quizzically.

She gave him the name of the hotel she was staying at in Naples as questions flew around her mind. "Sorry, I don't know where it is. I've lost the address, but I am sure the taxi drivers will know where to go." She closed her eyes. Yet another thing in her rucksack, although Phil would have retrieved it by now.

They made arrangements to share a taxi to the port on Tuesday morning and he added the name of her hotel into his schedule on his laptop.

"Tom?" Her heart was in her throat. She was about to make a huge fool of herself. He turned to her and frowned as she chewed her lip nervously.

"Yes?"

Bloody hell, could she do this?

She reached up and kissed him lightly, and as her lips brushed his stubbled cheek a tingle shot down her spine and she shivered.

Yes, it was about her only solution.

"Tom? Ah . . . Tom, would you consider marrying me?"

"What?" He looked at her for a moment. If it hadn't been so serious, the look on his face would have been enough to make her burst out laughing.

"You're quite serious, aren't you, Brianna?"

"Yes, I'm serious." The passengers around them began to stand and make their way down the aisle. He frowned and kept looking at her as though she was crazy.

"Look, just forget it for the time being. I'll tell you all about it when we catch the ferry on Tuesday. Okay? I'm not crazy. I'll have a proposition for you then."

Brianna stood and pushed past him, past caring that her backside was in his face as she stepped into the aisle.

"Just think about it. I'll see you later." She hurried down the aisle to where her laptop was stowed, anxious to get away from him before he could say no.

Problem number two. If Tom did say yes— and it was a long shot—if he did say yes, the next problem would be finding some way to repay him.

Chapter Five

Tom had booked a taxi through the concierge when he checked out from the hotel and now he gave the driver the address of Brianna's hotel. Unexpected anticipation curled in his stomach. He'd enjoyed exploring Naples and visiting Pompeii, and now he was looking forward to Lipari. He wondered how Brianna had spent the past couple of days. No doubt he would hear about it all the way to the island. And hear more about her crazy proposal.

He shook his head. This trip was far removed from his expectations. He was used to things going exactly as he'd planned. Maybe that's where he'd been going wrong? Once he found out why she needed a husband he would decide if she was plain crazy or if it was her ideas made her seem that way.

He'd slept soundly on Sunday night when he'd arrived on the flight from Rome and stepped out early on Monday to explore. No time to succumb to jet lag. Tomas was determined to enjoy every moment. Being able to speak the language had eased his way in Naples considerably, and he'd taken to the city like a native and had the strangest feeling of coming home. Their mother had encouraged them to appreciate their Italian heritage throughout their childhood, but apart from learning the language at home and then polishing it at university, he'd never been much interested in Italian culture. He enjoyed his mother's Italian cooking and he made sure he ate at home as often as he could, but now he was giving some thought to her belief that genetic memory played a big part in a person's cultural make up. He could get to like this place. He'd even become accustomed to the aroma of fish and garlic that pervaded every street.

It was less than a week since he'd left his office and already it felt like a different life. He'd not planned his day and had wandered around Naples as the mood had caught him and experienced the colours, flavours, and delights of this amazing city, visiting the Norman Castle, *Nuovo* and the *Castello del l'Ovo*. He'd taken the whole afternoon to spend time in the famous *Duomo* and the *Gesu Nuovo Church*. Even if he'd had to turn around and go home today, the richness of his experience in Naples had satisfied him already and he was looking forward to getting to Lipari Island.

Being alone in Italy had been most conducive to thinking, and as he'd explored, he'd given a lot of thought to what he was really doing here. The only downside had been the call from Nick.

"Hey, how's Italy?" he'd asked.

"Great," said Tom. "As much as I've seen in one day. I just got here."

"Rang to give you a heads up, mate."

"Heads up?"

"Mama and Aunt Carmen. They've been matchmaking. Looks like a bevy of hot Italian beauties may be lined up waiting for you at Aunt Carmen's apartment."

"Oh no. Please tell me you're kidding."

"Well, there's at least one coming for dinner the night you arrive. Some friend of the family. I got that much out of Mama after you left. Now that one of us is married, they're determined to set you up next."

"Thanks for the warning, appreciate it."

Tom groaned and finished the call. Nick's warning was welcome and he'd have to have a quiet word with his aunt. He was here to work . . . and then he smiled as he remembered the list he'd written on the flight. There would be time for some fun, but on his terms not anyone else's.

A blaring horn interrupted his thoughts and he grabbed for the door as the taxi driver wrenched the wheel to avoid yet another collision. One thing he would never get used to in Naples was the traffic. He closed his eyes and prayed he'd stay alive long enough to get to the ferry, as the taxi driver continued through the heavy traffic, beeping his way to their destination.

***

The phone line was filled with static and Brianna ran her free hand through her hair in frustration, before picking up the phrase book once more. It had taken the secretary from the Liparian law firm, *Antoniolli and Bruni*, two days to return her call. Luckily Phil had managed to get her rucksack back from the taxi company and she'd transferred their phone number to her laptop. At the rate she was spending money on phone calls, she'd have no money left to stay on Lipari for long.

Let alone pay someone to be her fiancé.

She had called the law firm twice yesterday, only to be told *Signore* Antoniolli was out and would call as soon as he returned. Anyway, that was what she thought the secretary was telling her. The language barrier on the phone was problematic. It was fine when you were face to face with someone. A nod and a smile and a phrase book had eased her way through the city these last couple of days.

Now, thanks to the dense secretary at *Antoniolli and Bruni*, she was running late for checkout. Tom would be waiting in a taxi and the silly woman on the other end wouldn't even try to understand. Brianna was using the phrase book in an attempt to communicate with the woman.

"*Il mio nome è Brianna. Signorina* Brianna, not *Signore* Brian. Look, I'll be there tomorrow." She scrabbled through the pages. "*Domani*, okay?"

The woman finally seemed to understand, and Brianna terminated the connection and headed for the elevator. Thank goodness she'd packed early and sent her bags down. Striding across to the checkout, she scanned the foyer for Tom and breathed a sigh of relief when he wasn't waiting.

At least she wasn't late. One thing had gone her way this morning and her checkout followed without a problem. Moving across to the glassed entrance she waited and tried not to worry about the conversation with the secretary. She doubted if the woman had understood her, and she was going to have to turn up on spec tomorrow. Surely someone there would be able to translate. She'd have to wait and see.

A white taxi sped into the drop off area at the front of the hotel and screeched to a halt. Tom leaned across and spoke to the driver before he opened the door and stepped out.

A warm feeling shot through her when he walked across the foyer toward her. Faded jeans clung to powerful thighs that the suit pants hadn't done any justice to at all, and a loose T-shirt proclaimed *Real Men Wear Jeans.*

Brianna stood on her toes and greeted him with a kiss on his smooth, clean-shaven cheek, and inhaled expensive cologne. "Mm, yummy . . . been shopping?"

He smiled down at her, looking relaxed and

more carefree than the formal man she had shared the flight with. He gestured down to his clothes. "These old rags? Na. Had 'em forever."

"No, I meant the *Silvestri*. I know my colognes."

"Well, I did fit in time for some shopping between sightseeing." He stepped back and looked at her. "It's a beautiful city. How about you? Did you get some sightseeing in?"

Brianna returned his steady gaze. His hair was mussed and his eyes were bright.

Much happier than the stranger on the plane. She'd had glimpses of this man as they had shared stories and was pleased to see how happy and relaxed he appeared.

"No. I stayed around here. Caught up on some work and tried to sort some business stuff out. With no luck, I'm afraid." She reached over and held his wrist up and looked down at his watch. "Come on, I'll tell you all about it on the ferry. We're running out of time."

Tom raised his eyebrows at her and grinned. "That's my line."

When the taxi dropped them off at the ferry terminal, she watched thoughtfully as Tom conversed with the driver in fluent Italian when he paid the fare. His snug jeans hugged his rear. He was in pretty good shape for someone who sat behind a desk all day.

Go slow. Italy might be the place for romance, but she needed him to pretend to be her fiancé first.

Forget the romance. You don't need it, girl.

***

The large inter-island ferry departed late from the busy marina and when they were finally underway, Tom stood beside her on the deck as Naples disappeared into the distance. It was a five-hour trip and they would dock about eight in the evening. Brianna planned to find a hotel room when they got there. In her usual 'trust in the gods' fashion, she hadn't booked, but she wasn't going to let that slip. Tom was going straight to his aunt's apartment. "I'll spend a couple of days there with her and then find myself an apartment."

They stood together and watched the Italian shoreline disappear in the heat haze. The smell of diesel and the cool spray forced them into the saloon of the ferry with the rest of the passengers. All of the seats were taken and they stood along the wall of the large cabin, occasionally grabbing the safety bar around the wall as the ferry ploughed through the rough swell.

"Drink?" Tom asked.

"Yes, please. I packed some snacks because I read there's not much food available on the ferry, but there is a bar."

Tom rejoined her with a bottle of red wine

and a couple of plastic cups. They moved through to the smaller lounge area where there was a vacant table and settled comfortably. Brianna delved into a plastic bag and spread some cheese and crackers on a plastic plate.

"Miss Organised," Tom said with a smile.

"See, some of your organising must have rubbed off on me because I'm usually pretty hopeless at thinking ahead. Don't get too used to it." She smiled apologetically. "The next couple of days are going to be a testament to that." Even though she'd been cross at him and his reaction—or more his lack of reaction when she'd proposed to him—she was grateful he hadn't mentioned her crazy proposal yet. "Can I tell you a story?"

"Certainly." Although he agreed, two small frown lines appeared between his eyebrows and she hastened to explain.

"I've got an appointment to see a lawyer tomorrow in Lipari to sort out some personal business." They both reached for their glasses at the same moment and their hands brushed. She smiled at him as the nerve endings tingled in her fingertips. "You know how I told you I come from a big family?"

He nodded again and held her gaze.

"Well, I'm adopted and I lived in Scotland with my adoptive family for most of my life. I tried to find my birth parents in my late teens, and Dad was understanding, but I think it bothered Mum a bit. She's been pretty upset with me about a few things."

"And did you find them?"

"Not then, and I got over it for a while. I went off to university and started my career and worked for a few years in England before going back home to Edinburgh to finish my Master's degree. Then I did my clinical training and started work."

Tom looked at her intently. "How old are you? You don't look old enough to have done all that."

"Thirty-one. I was always the odd one out with my olive skin and dark hair in a family of freckled redheads. Now I know it's my Italian background."

"You've found your family, then? That's why you're going to Lipari?" He spoke slowly. "Has that got anything to do with wanting to marry me?"

Brianna laughed. "Oh Tom. I don't want to marry you. I don't want to marry anybody . . . ever. But I have to, or at least I need a fiancé."

Before he could answer she rushed on, trying to speak clearly. She knew her accent made her difficult to understand when she got emotional.

And she was not going to get emotional.

"I'd only just arrived in Sydney when I got

a letter from an Italian law firm. It's chased me around the world. Scotland to England, and then it got emailed it to me when I was at the hotel in Sydney. It said my birth mother was recently deceased and I'm the beneficiary of her cottage in Lipari, but I have to claim it by the end of the month, a couple of days from now."

"You've certainly cut it close."

"That's why I had to cancel all my plans and fly over straight away. I have until this Friday to claim the cottage. There are some conditions attached to the inheritance."

"What sort of conditions?"

"That's another favour I want to ask you. I can't get through to them at the law office. I've had five different conversations with them, twice in Sydney and three times from Naples." She looked up at him, hoping fervently he would be happy to help her out. "How would you feel about coming with me and translating for me at the lawyer's tomorrow morning? You do speak the language like a native."

A shaft of red sunlight hit the wall behind him and she jumped up and grabbed his hand. "Come on. The sun's setting over the Tyrrhenian Sea. We can't miss that."

He gathered up the cups and leftover food, and put them back into the plastic bag she'd left on the seat and then followed her out to the deck. The breeze was cool and they stood close together as the sun dropped low in the sky. One by one, the other passengers gave in to the cold breeze and headed back into the warmth of the saloon. Brianna shivered and rubbed her arms.

"I didn't think to pack a coat. Summer in the Mediterranean, I thought it would be warmer."

"It's always cool out on the water." Tom removed his jacket and placed it around her shoulders. Her skin absorbed the lingering warmth from his jacket. His fingers brushed her throat as he pulled it around her and she shivered again. *But not from the cold.*

"Happy to stay out here till sunset? It's not far off now," he said. He stood behind her and put his arms loosely around her grasping the rail in front of them. She appreciated the warmth of his body blocking the chilly breeze blowing across the deck. They watched as the blood-red rays of the setting sun tinged the clouds with shades of colour ranging from the palest pink to silver. The last sliver of the orb dropped behind the water to the west and the wind dropped almost immediately.

"Would all their colours from the sunset take, from something of material sublime, rather than shadow our own soul's day-time in the dark void of night," Tom murmured.

"John Keats? You are full of surprises, Mr. Bursar." Brianna looked back at him and the wind

57

caught her loose strands of hair and blew it into his face.

"Sorry." She turned around, reached up, and removed the hair stuck to his cheek and was surprised by an intent look on his face before he dipped his head and caught her lips with the soft warmth of his. It caught her by surprise, and she stood stiff in his arms not sure how to respond. By the time she'd come to terms with it, he'd pulled back.

"You looked sad," he said with a smile. "And I couldn't resist trying to cheer you up. And, yes, I'll help you out. I'll come along to the lawyer and translate. Now, come back inside where it's warmer and you can tell me more about this visit to the lawyer's office and what you need me to find out." Tom held out his arm and waited for her to take it. "Oh, and perhaps while we're talking, maybe you can tell me if this has anything to do with your crazy proposal on the plane."

Brianna took his arm and looked up into serious blue eyes. She had a feeling she'd been set up. Sucked in by poetry and a kiss.

The last hour of the trip was rough and Brianna's stomach roiled as the ferry ploughed through the waves. A number of times she'd thought she would have to run for the bathroom, but fought it back. And it wasn't because of the conversation they'd just had. She blamed the cheese, wine, and the rough seas.

When she had come clean and told him why she needed a fake fiancé, he'd sat back without speaking for a few minutes and looked at her with narrowed eyes.

"For how long?"

"I don't know any more until I see the lawyer, and that's why I need you to translate so I get all the facts right."

"So, let me get this straight." His eyes were fixed on her face. "You need someone to pretend to be your fiancé so you can inherit your real mother's house, but you don't know anything more than that?"

She gulped and nodded. He was looking at her as though she was a wayward child.

Leaning forward, he nodded at her and a strange smile tilted his lips. "I think I can accommodate you. It might suit me fine to turn up with a fiancée on my arm."

Much to Brianna's amazement, he seemed to be considering her proposal and didn't tell her she was mad. She still couldn't believe it. If it wasn't for the look on his face, she might have said he felt sorry for her. She looked up into his closed face as he ran his hand through his short, cropped dark hair. There was no pity there.

"So you thought you'd call in to the local

employment agency and hire an actor?" He shook his head, obviously unable to believe anyone could be so stupid.

"No, I wasn't. There's no need to be rude," she snapped as her temper began to build. "It's my problem and I would have thought of something. You don't have to do it, Tom."

"Something?" He laughed. "Anyway, I keep my word. I've agreed to help you out and I will. I don't want any surprises when we get there. I want the complete truth."

"There's no more to tell. I apparently need a husband before I can inherit the cottage, and the why remains a mystery. That's what I'll . . . we'll . . . be finding out tomorrow."

Diesel fumes filled the saloon and Tom got up and closed the door to the deck. They sat without speaking as the ferry pounded through the heavy seas around the Aeolian Islands, before turning into a quiet harbour. The waves calmed and she began to feel better as the ferry glided across the still water. The moonlight shone on the rainbow slick of the oily water as the ferry berthed at the marina on Lipari Island

They presented their tickets and collected their bags from the luggage bay and disembarked. Brianna was grateful for Tom's hand underneath her elbow as they walked down the slippery ramp to the boardwalk dragging their suitcases behind them.

Despite his arrogance, he could be polite and thoughtful.

When it suited him.

He slung both their laptop bags across his shoulders so Brianna could hold the railing with her other hand. As soon as they stepped onto the boardwalk her stomach settled and her mood improved.

Things would work out. Something would happen. It always had for her.

The narrow ramp led across to a cobblestoned corso covered with stalls, and a night market festooned with fairy lights was in full swing. She looked up in delight at bunches of wildflowers hanging in garlands around the first two stalls.

"Oh, look at those gorgeous colours!" Leaning her suitcase against a stone wall, she scrabbled in her money belt and instructed Tom to mind her bag. She made her purchase and walked back over to him, holding the sweet smelling flowers up to her face. "Come on, let's explore," she said excitedly.

He shook his head with a frown.

"We'll take your bag to your hotel first so you don't have to cart your luggage around. Where are you staying?"

She swallowed and looked up at him. "Don't know yet. Wherever I can find a hotel room, I suppose."

"You mean you haven't booked anywhere?" The exasperation was clear on his face and she glared at him.

Who did he think he was?

"Chill out, it's not your worry. After I've looked at the market, I'll go and find something. Don't be such a stuffed shirt. I'm in Italy and I plan to enjoy every second, no matter what happens."

"Brianna," he said in a condescending tone. "There are times to be responsible and then you can have fun. You'll enjoy yourself even more."

"Who says?" She put her hands on her hips and stood nose to nose with him. Or at least she attempted to. It was more nose to chest. She was tall and he still towered over her.

"I say," he said firmly. "Now, come on, we'll find you a hotel."

"But . . . " She stumbled over her words and tried to think of a suitable retort, but he took her arm and marched her up the hill away from the tempting market stalls. A small brightly-lit hotel was situated at the top overlooking the wharf and he ushered her through the doorway.

"You book in. Then we can get something to eat, and then I'll find my aunt's apartment." He gave her a tight smile. "That way I'll know where to find you so I can accompany you to your appointment tomorrow."

She glared at him without replying.

Accompany me to my appointment. Jesus, how about you come with me.?

"That's if you're still talking to me and want me to translate for you," he said as a grin crossed his face. "Oh, and if you still need that fiancé."

She gritted her teeth and made her way to the counter to ask if there was a room. If she wanted him to help her, she was going to have to put up with him taking charge, and that did not sit well with her.

When the young girl on reception told her she was lucky to get the last room because it was festival time on the island, she nodded and filled in the registration form, determined not to let Tom know he was right. Being independent had never failed her before, and she was certainly not going to start relying on someone now to get her organised. And she hadn't expected, or appreciated, the warm fuzzy feeling that had filled her chest when he'd shortened her name. Putting the key in her pocket, she walked across to him, leaving her bags at the reception counter.

"All sorted," she said forcing a carefree tone into her voice. "Don't worry about staying with me. I'm going to grab something to eat at the market and have a bit of a look around. There's no appointment time set for tomorrow, so turn up here whenever it suits you."

Regret settled in her stomach like a brick

when he simply nodded at her, and handed her the laptop bag, his face expressionless. She watched until the dark swallowed him, and then asked the receptionist if she could arrange to have her luggage sent up. Forcing a jauntiness she didn't feel into her step, she headed down the hill to the night market. Even though he pushed her buttons, Tom's sense of responsibility had made things a little easier.

She could get quite comfortable having him around, despite his smartarse attitude.

Chapter Six

Tom's quiet swearing was muffled by the music and noise of the market as he headed back down the hill. He'd be damned if he was going to turn around and check if she was all right. She was *not* his responsibility.

God, she hadn't even booked a room, he thought. Talk about irresponsible. He didn't need any complications in his life. He was here to enjoy himself and not worry about someone who couldn't organise themselves. "Well, stop worrying about a grown woman you just met who is quite capable of looking after herself," said the little devil in his thoughts.

"Shit." He didn't think she could look after herself. If the conversation he had overheard with her brother was anything to go by, she couldn't even look after her possessions. And he knew what his real problem was—he found her way too attractive and too fascinating for his own good. When she'd buried her face in those bloody flowers and looked up at him, he'd been tempted to kiss her again. And that was the last thing he needed. Why on earth had he kissed her on the boat?

Sprouting Keats and kissing her?

She'd already said she thought he was a

right . . . what did she call him? A right balloon. Well, he'd confirmed it for her now. He hadn't even thought about it before he'd kissed her. It'd just happened, and he was damned if he was going to lose sleep over a single kiss. In fact, he'd probably lose sleep because he couldn't get her out of his mind. And not just her problems either. The warmth of her body lingered on his skin and his heart gave a little jump.

"Nothing wrong with a good time," said the little voice. "After all, you *are* here to start your new life.

He reached the end of the street and turned right. The cathedral was on the left as he remembered, and then he passed the *Museo Archeologico* before turning back toward the harbour where Carmen's apartment was located adjacent to the small marina she and Uncle Renzo had inherited from his grandparents.

A wave of nostalgia washed over him as he turned into the street and headed toward the bright blue door of Aunt Carmen's apartment. He had played in this street as a child with his brothers and sisters when they had visited from Australia. The balcony on the first floor still had the same table and chairs and hanging plants of his childhood memories. His parents and aunt and uncle had sat up there in the early evening and watched them all playing in the street below. He shrugged off thoughts of his new

Scottish friend and her problems. Dealing with his reaction to Brianna could wait till tomorrow. He had his own life to sort out first.

The entry to the apartment was at street level overlooking the marina and the office was next door. The signage to the business was faded, and there was no information about opening hours or services available. Even as he raised his hand to ring the bell, his mind ticked over. True, he knew very little about running a marina, but good business practice carried across, no matter what the enterprise was. He would have to talk to the staff about getting some advertising out there for catching the passing tourist trade.

Before he could press the buzzer, the door opened and he was assailed by the overpowering smell of rose perfume and an excited squeal. He dropped his suitcase and held out his arms as Aunt Carmen reached out, and grabbed his cheeks with her soft, plump hands, pulling his head down for an exuberant kiss on both sides of his face.

"Oh, Tomas, look how you have grown!"

He grinned. Of course he had—he hadn't visited Lipari Island since he was a teenager. It had been years since he'd last seen his aunt, but his childhood memories of spending time with Carmen and Renzo were wonderful. Before his father had taken the professorship in Armidale, his parents had traveled the world, and he had spent several summers on this beautiful island with his family. But it had been fifteen years since his last visit and now Uncle Renzo had passed on. Tom took his aunt's arm and stood back. She had aged and he was pleased he could help out and keep the business in the family.

"It is wonderful to be here, Aunt Carmen. "

"Come in, come in. I have someone I want you to meet." She chattered on as she led him into the small entry foyer. Tom picked up his bags and followed her down the narrow hallway.

"Put your bags in my room. You will be sleeping in the pull-down bed in the living room until I leave."

"Leave?"

"I am going on a trip. You will need somewhere to sleep, so you will have my bed after I leave tomorrow."

She led him into her bedroom, and Tom closed his eyes as the smell of roses mixed with camphor and mold hit him. Opening them and looking around, his stomach sank. The walls were papered in huge pink roses and on the east-facing wall a small shrine protruded out into the middle of the room. Tom placed his bags next to the table, which was filled with candles, rosaries, holy cards, and a huge photograph of Uncle Renzo. Incense burned in a small brass receptacle and his stomach moved toward his throat at the mix of the cloying smells.

"You will be able to pray in here as well." Aunt Carmen beamed at him and pointed to the prayer cushion on the floor.

Tom thought of his minimalist apartment back home overlooking the park in Armidale, with its white walls and lightly polished floors. And he hadn't been to a church since his mother had dragged him along to his confirmation over twenty years ago.

"Ah, yes. Thank you, but I will be staying with my…er…fiancé."

Aunt Carmen's face fell. "Your fiancé?"

"Yes, Brianna and I became engaged on the trip over." There was no need to tell his aunt they'd only met on the trip over as well. No one needed to know the background of this fake engagement it looked like he had decided to agree to and he'd sort out something to tell his family when he thought of it.

"If you're talking to Mama, please don't mention it yet. We haven't told anyone." Tom swallowed.

"You're the first to know, Aunt Carmen."

"And I'm the second."

As they walked into the small kitchen, a young woman stood and held her hand out to Tom. Dressed in a low-cut red dress, which showed her ample cleavage, she looked him up and down and he sensed he was found wanting.

"Tomas, this is Helena. She will be your secretary in the office from tomorrow."

"Oh, good." Tom took her hand and shook it. "You can show me around and help me get set up."

"No," she said, boredom lacing her voice. "It is my first day too."

Tom turned to his aunt and she shrugged. "Ah, I thought it would be nice for you to have someone in the office with you... and Helena is my friend's daughter and she was looking for a job."

"Oh, I see." Tom wondered if Helena was one of the women Nick had mentioned on the phone.

Aunt Carmen gestured for him to sit at the table. Despite the smells in the rest of the apartment, the aroma coming from the pots on the stove was mouth-watering.

As his aunt served their meal, Tom tried to converse with Helena, but she had picked up a nail file and was filing her long red fingernails with disinterest and avoided looking at him. After a few questions to her, which she ignored, he turned to his aunt and caught her up with the family news. It was difficult to focus on the conversation, and he tried to keep his thoughts away from Brianna, but all he could see was the cross look on her face when he'd left her at the hotel. As well as those legs that went forever, Christ, he was the one who should be cross. Bloody crazy scheme and now he'd committed to it by telling his aunt he had a fiancé.

"Well, Tomas?" He realised his aunt had asked him a question.

"Are you staying here tonight? You have brought your luggage, but not your fiancé?"

"Sorry, Aunt Carmen, I must be a bit jet lagged. I'll stay here tonight with you and then Brianna and I will look for an apartment tomorrow."

God, this was becoming more complicated by the minute. Why the hell had he promised to help Brianna out?

***

Brianna sat in the warm sun, her back

against the whitewashed wall of the small hotel where she'd spent the night. Her booted feet were crossed in front of her and the sun warmed her bare legs. A good night's sleep had put her in a much better frame of mind. Things were looking up. Tom would translate for her, and until she saw what the deal was with the inheritance, the lawyers would see she had a husband in the making.

She owed Tom an apology for losing her temper and being a smart-mouthed bitch last night. After all, there was really no reason for him to help her out. It wasn't as if they were even friends. She wondered why he'd agreed.

I'll hold my temper in and not say a thing, even when he does act like a jerk. She grinned when she remembered how he'd reacted last night and left her standing there. She hadn't stayed long at the market, just wandered around the cobbled streets wondering whether her mother had ever walked on the same streets at some time in her life.

She sighed. There was so much to find out and so many questions to be answered.

If Tom hadn't been coming with her this morning, she would have been in a right state by now. But knowing he'd be there had eased her mind a little. She'd slept soundly and was looking forward to sorting out the legal details, and hopefully seeing her mother's cottage. Maybe they'd even have some pictures and personal effects, something to help her know her mother.

"*Cassetta*," she corrected herself. Time to start learning the language.

It was a moment she'd waited a long time for, and she couldn't believe how close she'd come to losing it. If she hadn't made the call from Sydney saying she would be here by the end of the week, she would have missed out and the house would have gone to someone else. So there had to be more family somewhere. A shiver of excitement rippled through her. She'd tried for so long to find out about her mother. She wondered if Rosa had been born here or if she had moved here alone. It wouldn't be long now and all would be revealed . . . hopefully.

She sighed. The news about the inheritance had been totally unexpected and she hadn't had much time to think about what it was going to mean for her life. There were some big changes coming, of that she was sure.

The crunch of footsteps on the white gravel leading to the hotel entrance caught her attention, and she looked across the brightly coloured garden. Tom was striding through the gate and she pushed herself to her feet as he crossed the small patch of lawn toward her.

"Good morning." She injected as much enthusiasm as she could into her voice. "Isn't it the most sparkly day?" Lifting her arm, she shaded her eyes and pointed to the harbour where teenagers were tacking across the ruffled water in small yachts with madly flapping sails. "Look."

The morning sunlight reflected off the small waves stirred up by the light breeze as the yachts bounced along. The shrill cries of the young sailors carried across the water and were overlaid by the deep booming of the morning ferry's horn as it pulled away from the wharf for the trip back to the mainland.

"It certainly is a beautiful morning," said Tom. Despite agreeing with her, his voice was clipped, and she sensed he was still cross with her. They stood together for a moment watching the boats whiz across the bay before he turned toward the road without speaking again.

"I love this island already," Brianna said as she followed Tom out through the gate. "Everyone is so friendly. I chatted to at least half a dozen people as I waited," she added with a smile. "Well, I talked to them anyway. I didn't understand a word they said, but they were all very friendly." She held up her guidebook. "But I'm learning phrases."

Tom walked along beside her quietly as they climbed the hill to the main part of the small town, and she tried to keep a conversation going. That is if one-sided prattle with monosyllabic replies could be called conversation. If he was cross with her he could go to hell and she would cope. No one was going to spoil the day she found out about her mother. Something would happen. Trust in the universe.

"How is your aunt?"

"Well." He surprised her with not only an answer, but it was accompanied with a smile. "Aunt Carmen is a smaller version of my mother, but just as vivacious."

"I love that word," said Brianna. "Do you know the Italian for it?"

Tom glanced across at her, but she couldn't read his expression in the shadows of the shaded street.

"Very close to the English. *Vivace*."

"*Vivace*." The word rolled off her tongue, and she tried to stop her Scottish burr. "I'm picking up the language." When he didn't reply, she glanced back at him. "Even though she is *vivace*, is everything else okay? You looked like the weight of the world was on your shoulders as you came in the gate. Or is it because you are still cross with me?" She needed to clear the air before they got to the lawyer's office. After all, they were playing the role of an engaged couple in love.

He stopped and answered her with a sort of humph.

"And no, I'm not psycho-analysing you," she said. "You have to get over that perception. I've been good at picking up people's feelings since I was a child, and all my friends used to spill their souls to me. It's one of the reasons I went into psychology."

She grabbed his arm and pulled him to a stop beside her. 'Tom!'

"I'm not cross with you," he said.

"Well now, if you're not cross with me, at least be up front with me. I can tell there is something bugging you. Have you changed your mind about coming with me? Are you worried about me taking advantage of you? Are you scared you're going to appear in my book?" She stared up at him. "But for goodness sake talk to me. Get it over with and then I can sort something else out."

God, how on earth would she really cope without any knowledge of Italian? She'd had enough trouble with the secretary on the phone. She'd rushed to get here and she hadn't even thought to buy a phrase book, and her trusty guide book only had the most basic phrases in it. Then she saw the funny side of it and giggled . . . at least she could say hello and goodbye and where's the toilet?

"No, I made a commitment to you," Tom said and she smothered a smile. They were a fine pair. She couldn't speak Italian and his language was so formal.

"I'm coming with you, and no, I'm not worried that you will take advantage of me." He started walking up the hill and looked back at her over his shoulder. "And I hadn't even given any thought to appearing in your book. I'm certainly not interesting enough to appear in a psychology book."

But his formal language might come in very handy in the lawyer's office, she thought.

"I'm thinking about how we'll handle it. I'm sorry if I don't indulge in mindless chatter just for the sake of having a conversation."

The comment wiped away the grin that had been pulling at her mouth, and turned it into a cough.

Mindless chatter, indeed. Well, she could play intellectual, no conversation games, too.

If only she didn't find him so damned attractive it would be a lot easier. Every time he stood close to her, she got a whiff of his citrusy aftershave, and a sharp insistent tug of desire shot through her. *Again.*

"Aunt Carmen had prepared a room for me and wants me to move in, but her place is no bigger than a shoe box. She had to move some furniture to get the fold-out bed down for me last night." He laughed and rubbed his back. "My feet hung over the end of the bed all night." As soon as we see your lawyer, I have to get back to the marina. My aunt is leaving for the mainland. I'd like you to come too because she wants to meet my fiancé."

Brianna stopped and Tom turned around and looked at her with exasperation.

"Jeez, you told somebody we were engaged?" she said. "It would be best if we keep it as quiet as possible."

"Yes, but it's a two-way street. It suits me well to have a fiancée too."

Relief coursed through Brianna. If he needed her as much as she needed him, there was a better chance of it all working out. She walked around in front of him and stood on her tiptoes. Ever since he'd come through the gate, she'd been watching his mouth when he spoke. Now she gave in to the impulsive urge that had been tugging at her and reached up and kissed him.

"Happy engagement."

Ignoring the warmth that filled her as she touched his lips, she pulled back and smiled at him before taking his hand. "Come on then, we'll get my legal stuff over and sorted and then we'll ask around in town and see if we can find you somewhere to live on the way back to your aunt's." She squeezed his hand. "I was so worried you'd changed your mind about coming with me."

"I don't go back on my word. You can trust me."

Brianna wiped her forearm across her forehead. When they stepped into the town square from the cool shade of the buildings in the back streets, the mid-morning sun was belting down. She reached up with one finger and wiped a line of perspiration from Tom's top lip.

"I thought an Aussie boy would be used to the heat."

"I live in the highlands. Cold winters and temperate summers."

She reached into her bag and then dabbed at her face with a tissue. "We're a fine pair. You know what they say about mad dogs and Englishmen. Make it a Scotswoman!"

"Which way?" asked Tom. Old brick buildings lined the footpath around the edge of the square.

Brianna swallowed nervously and looked around. "Umm . . . I'm not quite sure."

She pointed across the square. "Maybe that way?"

Tom looked back at her with a quizzical smile. "What's the address?"

"I don't actually know."

He turned with his hands on his hips. "You don't know? You've travelled across the world and you don't know where you're going?"

Despite his body language indicating otherwise, his voice was patient and it really annoyed her. "Of course I do. I know the name of the firm. It's *Antoniolli and Bruni*. I just don't have the address."

"Wasn't it on the letter they sent you?"

"Yes, Mr. Twenty Questions. It was . . . but I . . . ah . . . I haven't got it with me." Irritation burned in her stomach when Tom looked at her, disbelief written all over his face.

"Well, we'll have to go back and get it." He grabbed her shoulders and turned her back toward her hotel, and looked at her with those sexy lips set in a straight line when she didn't start walking.

"Hurry up, or we'll be late," he said patiently.

"No we won't. I don't have an appointment either, remember." Sarcasm laced her voice while she tried to forget about how his lips had felt on hers. "And I suppose you're never late for anything, are you? I'd take bets on that."

"Look, do you want me to help you with this or not? I can quite easily spend my time finding an apartment. I'm happy to help, but I can't unless we actually get there."

"I'm sorry. Look, I didn't mean to snap. It's just you are so bloody perfect. I know where to go, we simply have to ask someone where it is because I . . . lost the letter." Her face heated when the realisation dawned on his face.

"Lost it? Where?"

"It's in Sydney. It's a long story." She looked around and noticed a small store across the street. "It's not a problem. I'll sort it out."

Leaving him standing on the footpath,

Brianna stepped into the grocery store and smiled at the short, stout woman behind the counter. Garlands of flowers hung in profusion along each side of the counter, and strands of garlic bulbs were threaded along the front of the counter. Jars of plump olives in all sorts of different coloured marinades tempted her. A huge tub full of the biggest avocadoes she had ever seen sat by the counter. For a moment she stood and inhaled the mixture of aromas, and then Tom's shadow filled the doorway and she scurried over to the counter.

"Ah . . . er . . . excuse me . . . er . . . *scusi.*" She was determined to show him she could do this without his help. The woman smiled at her. "Er... I need to find . . . Mr. Antoniollo . . . and er . . . *Signore* Bruni?

The woman tilted her head to the side *"Quale?"*

"Ah . . . *Signore* Antoniolli . . . the lawyer?"

The woman shrugged her shoulders and lifted both hands, palms turned upward in that expressive Mediterranean way. Tom stepped up behind her and placed his hand gently on her bare shoulder. Her skin burned under his hand as the nerve endings fired. He spoke in rapid Italian to the little lady, and Brianna looked at him in confusion when he said avocado.

What the hell was he doing?

She stepped away from his hand. The

woman laughed and replied *"Ah . . . si, avocatto."*

She stepped around the counter and took Tom by the hand, leading him across to the door before she pointed up the hill and appeared to give him directions with much waving of her free arm.

"Grazie." Tom reached into his pocket and slipped some money into the woman's hand before turning to Brianna.

"Come on, *Signores* Antoniolli and Bruni are up the hill and around the corner. His eyes crinkled at the edges. "And, Brianna, we may even be early for your non-appointment. They don't open until eleven o'clock."

The foyer of the law firm was a tiny room closed in with dark timber lining. A secretary sat at a small desk typing on an old-fashioned typewriter. Her fingers clattered on the keys and the bell rang when she pressed the carriage return with a flourish as she reached the end of a line. Brianna was fascinated to think that in this day and age they would have an old manual typewriter. And the old telephone handset on the desk was an old fashioned one with the numbers in a circular dial on the front.

Tom placed his hand on her back and the warmth shooting up her spine took her thoughts away from typewriters and telephones.

"Would you like me to handle this?" he asked.

She didn't need the warmth of his hand through the thin material of her spaghetti-strapped T-shirt. Her shoulder was still tingling from where he had placed his hand on her bare skin in the shop where she thought he'd had too much sun and had been buying avocados. She'd soon realised what was happening. *Avocatto* meant lawyer.

Vivace and *avocatto*. She was picking up the language quickly. At this rate, she'd be fluent by the end of the week and wouldn't need Tom to translate.

"Thank you." She didn't want to appear rude. After all, he was helping her and she would certainly find this much more difficult if she hadn't had the good fortune to meet him on the plane. Maybe he wasn't such a stuffed shirt after all. There was something to be said for being organised and planning ahead. He'd made her morning a lot easier. If it wasn't for him, she'd still be wandering around trying to find the blasted law firm. Reaching up, she took his hand and squeezed it gently.

His fingers gripped hers and those sexy, crinkly lines appeared around his eyes.

"My pleasure. We'll get you organised in no time."

She laughed softly before she replied. "Don't hold your breath. My family has been trying to do that for thirty years." She tilted her head to the side. "They don't call me Brianna. They call me lightning."

Before he could reply, the office door opened and a small man with white hair and a deeply lined face reached out and grabbed Tom's hand and shook it vigorously.

"*Signore Ballantyne, benvenuto . . . benvenuto.* He peered over the top of his little round glasses at Brianna and smiled at her. "*Signora Ballantyne?*"

He nodded his head and he kept smiling as he pumped Tom's hand. Tom began to speak, and the old lawyer raised his hand and stopped him.

"*Un momento.*"

He turned to the secretary, and pointed to the telephone. "*Signore Caranto*," he said before ushering them ahead of him into his office.

A small lamp on the side of the desk shone onto the huge timber desk and provided the only light in the dim office. The heavy dark drapes were drawn, blocking out the morning sunshine. Brianna wrinkled her nose. The smell of mould was overpowering and she blinked her eyes trying to ignore the claustrophobia that crept over her. The elderly lawyer ushered them to seats in front of the desk, and Tom waited till she was seated before taking the chair beside her.

Tom and the elderly lawyer chatted for some minutes, and Brianna gave up trying to follow the gist of the fast-paced conversation, but it all seemed very social. There was a tap on the door and the secretary appeared with a tray of coffee and biscuits. All was quiet as she poured coffee for them.

Tom glanced across at her and when she returned his gaze, Brianna caught sight of another elderly man who must have followed the secretary into the room. He sat silently across the room in a chair in the dark corner. She nudged Tom and a look of surprise crossed his face as he also realised there was a fourth person in the room

Probably Mr . . . no, start thinking Italian, she corrected herself.

Probably *Signore* Bruni.

Signore Antoniolli paid no attention to the other lawyer and did not introduce him. He stood and crossed the room to a huge wooden filing cabinet and pulled out a sheaf of paper tied with string before launching into a lengthy conversation with Tom.

Tom participated in the discussion, intense concentration etched on his face. He seemed to be doing a lot of frowning, and the smile crinkles she loved looking at were replaced by deep lines on his forehead. Occasionally, he put up his hand to pause *Signore* Antoniolli and pointed to Brianna and asked a question of the lawyer.

She looked from one to the other and then placed her hand on Tom's arm. She wanted to know what was being said. Tom shook his head and the elderly lawyer frowned at her. A flash of white caught her eye and she looked across to the corner as the other lawyer wiped a tear from his eye. Absorbed in watching the old man wipe his eyes, she jumped when Tom reached out and placed his arm around her shoulder and pulled her close to him.

He leaned down and placed his lips against hers before she could move. "What the f—," she whispered against his lips.

"Just follow my lead," he murmured into her mouth.

"Kissing men, crying lawyers. This is bizarre," she muttered and Tom frowned at her.

She sat straight in her chair and flicked her braid over her shoulder. She concentrated and tried to follow the conversation. Signore Antoniolli directed a comment to the man in the corner, and he gave a cry of distress and jumped out of his chair, launching himself at her. He leaned over and hugged her tightly from behind, his papery skin rubbed against her cheek before he stood and wiped his eyes once again.

"*Più tardi*," he said as he walked to the door and left pulling it shut behind him.

Brianna turned to Tom, absolutely bewildered. "What the hell was that all about? Translate please."

"Later."

"No, now," she said in a furious whisper. "Tell me *now*."

Tom looked at her patiently. "It means later. *Più tardi* means later."

"Oh," she replied sheepishly. "Thank you."

The conversation continued around her and the lawyer slid some papers over for her to sign. She choked back a laugh when he passed her a fountain pen and gestured to the ink well. She looked up at Tom and he nodded.

"It's an acceptance of the conditions of the inheritance. You dip the nib in the ink," said Tom when she looked blankly at the old-fashioned pen.

"I know." She clenched her jaw. "What am I signing? Shouldn't I know first? Do I have to do it right now?"

"It's an acceptance of the deeds of your mother's house. It's called *la Casa Bianca* . . . the White House. The conditions are straightforward, but you need to sign them today." He dropped his voice to a whisper. "You've just made it by the skin of your teeth, Brianna. If you'd been one day later, the time for you to claim your inheritance would have run out and you would have had a huge legal battle on your hands."

"Oh," she said in a small voice. Tears filled her eyes and her chest tightened as emotion welled through her. Her hands shook as she dipped the pen in the ink well.

My mother. My real mother. Rosa's house.

She fought to stop her chin quivering as she signed the paper with shaking hands.

She'd had no idea it could be sorted so quickly. The lawyer smiled hugely when she pushed the papers across the desk to him. He went to a cupboard and pulled out a heavy brass key and handed it to Tom. Brianna's throat tightened and she swallowed. Her chest was heavy and this stuffy room was closing in on her

I have to get outside.

"Congratulazioni." Signore Antoniolli shook Tom's hand and then hers, before he ushered them through the door. *"Fino a domani."*

Brianna quickly walked out and Tom followed. The midday sunshine was bright and she covered her eyes, blinking back tears.

"Are you all right?"

"No," she said taking deep gulps of the welcome fresh air. "I'm starting to realise this is all true. It was an adventure when I got that letter and now—" she reached across and took the old key from Tom, "— I am holding the key to my mother's house."

She burst into tears, unable to hold the emotion back any longer.

***

Tom looked down at Brianna as she sobbed

and grasped the large key to her chest. He stepped over and put his arms around her and patted her awkwardly on the back. The loose hair that constantly unwound from her braid tickled his nose and the softness of her breasts pressed into his chest. He had been privy to Brianna's emotion since she had first squeezed past him on the plane. She was open and honest, and didn't seem to hold back no matter how she was feeling.

Even when she thought I was a jerk.

She leaned into him closely for a few seconds and then she stepped back with a muffled sniff, before childishly wiping her nose with the back of her hand. She held the key and turned it over and over, rubbing her long slender fingers against the gnarled edge. His heart kicked in sympathy as the tears rolled down her cheeks.

She wiped them away. "Okay, Mr. Italian speaker. Take me to my house." She smiled up at him through her tears. "I'm sure you asked for the address?"

Tom looked down at her.

"Yes, *Signore* Antoniolli gave me the address. It's actually in the next village and we have to catch the bus. The village is called Cannetto."

He ran his hand through his hair and turned away from her for a moment to gather his thoughts.

How the hell was she going to take the rest of the news he had to tell her?

The content of the conversation that had taken place in the office would floor her. It still floored him and he needed to take some time to digest what he had done himself.

He grabbed her hand and led her across the street. He'd really become a part of Brianna's adventures and had given little thought to the reason for his own visit. He had to get back to the marina later in the day, and he had to remember his commitments there. This feisty woman was in the forefront of his mind and he needed to pull back.

"Before we catch the bus, we need to sit down and have a coffee so I can tell you what happened. There were a . . . er . . . a few more legal things we have to organise."

"There's a café over there by the square." She pointed past the fountain to an outdoor café. "Come on, I want to hear everything." Keeping his hand gripped tightly in hers, Brianna marched toward the middle of the square, her boots pounding on the cobblestones as she dragged him along behind her. He glanced down and was far enough behind to admire the long tanned legs beneath her shorts before he caught up to her.

Tom shook his head. He had never before met a woman who was so sure of herself, yet so soft and emotional at the same time. She had layer upon layer of resilience, and he was getting a fascinating glimpse of her character each time she was presented with a challenge.

"And who was that crazy old man who grabbed me on his way out of the office?" she asked as they passed an old fountain with a statue of Neptune extending his arms in a lordly gesture of stilling the waters. "That was downright creepy. Strangest law firm I've ever been in."

"Ah… he was—" Tom cleared his throat, at a loss for words.

Just tell her.

"He's your grandfather."

Brianna stopped abruptly and Tom bumped into her almost pushing them both into the fountain.

"What did you say?"

"I said he is your grandfather. Come on, I'll tell you everything when we sit down."

By the time, they sat down and their coffee was brought to the table, Brianna appeared more composed. Her tanned face was unusually pale, and a little freckle he hadn't noticed before stood out on the side of her cheek. He reached over and took her hands in his, and a jolt of pleasure ran through him when she responded and tightly linked her fingers through his.

"*Signore* Antoniolli filled me in on your family background and the strict conditions of your inheritance. Now, tell me what you know first so I don't repeat it all."

Being devious didn't come naturally to him.

He needed to be sure she hadn't known the conditions of the will and he wasn't being conned. He remembered Nick telling him on many occasions that he was a soft touch. Too many women had tried to dupe him, making him look the fool.

"Hello?" Brianna tugged on his arm.

"Oh, sorry. Where were we?" He straightened in his chair and brought his mind back to the present. "Now, tell me what you know about your Liparian family."

"My Liparian family?"

Her Scottish burr and the Italian words were an interesting mix. He could listen to her soothing accent all day.

"Nothing, zero, zilch, I know nothing. The first I knew was the letter I got in Australia and when I rang the number they asked for Brian." She pulled one hand back from his and grabbed her braid. He was starting to recognise this was a sign she was nervous.

He took a deep breath wondering why the hell he'd done what he had.

Was he crazy? He'd had taken a lot upon himself in the lawyer's office and was more than a bit wary of her reaction, to say the least. Maybe he should have run it by her first, but he didn't want to give the lawyer any inkling that things weren't as he thought.

He'd come over here to loosen up and certainly hadn't expected to get married as soon as he arrived. Taking a deep breath, he prepared to tell her what he'd just promised the lawyer.

Chapter Seven

"You what?" Brianna looked at Tom wondering if he was the crazy one. "Did you just say we are getting married?" She pulled a tissue from her bag and wiped the last of her tears away.

Tom nodded.

"And you did say tomorrow?"

When he nodded a second time without speaking, she pushed her chair back and stood up.

"Whoa. I said I needed a fiancé, not a bloody husband." She strode out for the bus top across the square, not caring if he followed her or not.

"Brianna, wait." Tom hurried after her, catching her as she reached the bus stop. "Don't go getting yourself all worked up."

She looked up at the sign above the bus stop at the far end of the square. She could read the sign to the towns the bus visited and it said Cannetto so she was in the right place. At the moment, she didn't care if Tom was with her or not. Her temper was firing and she was having trouble being polite.

"Worked up? I asked you to pretend to be my fiancé and before I know it you've organised a whole bloody wedding with my lawyer without one word to me."

"Will you listen to me?" He spoke loudly as he grabbed her arm and she looked down with disdain. There was no one around to overhear them in the square was deserted. "Unless you signed that document today and also proved you were married, there was no way you would have got your mother's house. As it was, I had to do some quick thinking and assure him we were getting married straight away or you would have missed your chance."

She leaned against the warm brick wall and folded her arms and watched Tom. Her temper faded away and was replaced by a glimmer of sympathy as she appreciated what he'd done. Before she could speak the bus appeared around the corner and Tom put his hand out and held it as they walked over to the bus. After they boarded, he followed her to the back of the bus where there were two vacant seats.

Her shoulder rubbed against his as the old bus trundled up the steep hill to Cannetto, the village closest to Lipari. The spectacular view across the water from the top of the cliff filled the window as the bus lurched close to the edge of a big drop. Neither the sapphire-blue waters of the Mediterranean nor the profusion of wildflowers growing down the side of the cliff could hold her attention while she tried to process what Tom had just told her.

I have a grandfather and he wants to see me this afternoon.

And I have a house.

And Tom and I are getting married.

A giggle bubbled up from her chest and she fought to control it. He sat there beside her with no expression. He was a master at hiding what he was thinking, although he had been very intense when he'd held her hand and told her what had ensued in the lawyer's office. For some reason, she could see the humorous side of what he'd done. She choked it back and the tears welled in her eyes. He reached over and patted her arm.

"It's okay. I'll help you sort it out."

She leaned forward, her shoulders shaking from crying, and put her hands over her face. Tom rubbed her back, his warm hand etched soothing circles through her thin T-shirt, and her skin sizzled beneath his fingers.

"Come on." His voice sounded strained. "It's okay. We'll figure out a way to get around it. There's no need to cry." Brianna straightened up and looked across at him.

"I've had some amazing friends in my life and lots of people have done good things for me, but no one has ever stepped up for me like you did today." She leaned across and somehow his arm ended up around her and she was against his chest. "What you did was the most gracious and amazing thing. Now tell me all the details."

She laughed with sheer delight when he'd repeated what had been discussed in Signore Antoniolli's office. Then in his organised fashion he ticked off the things they needed: an *Atto Notorio* filled in at the town hall and faxed to the consulate, a statutory declaration, and their birth certificates. He had been amazed when she said she had a copy of her birth certificate in her travel documents.

"I carried it with me to Australia, in case I needed proof of identity over there. But surely he knows your aunt. It's such a small island. Wouldn't he have known you were coming over anyway? Is it too much of a coincidence?" She chewed her bottom lip.

"No." Tom paused for a moment. "There is something a bit tricky there, but nothing you need to worry about yet. I'll explain later, but he definitely didn't know either of us were coming until they rang him today." He leaned in closer, and Brianna got a whiff of his aftershave and stared back at him fascinated by the black rims around his deep blue irises. She hadn't noticed before what beautiful eyes he had.

"I knew I was taking a big risk telling him we were about to get married, but I couldn't risk telling you in the office, because he might have been a bit suspicious. Especially with your grandfather there."

"So—" She dragged her attention back to what he was saying. "You said we would be getting married soon just so I wouldn't lose the house? Why would you do that for me? It's not like you even really know me." She looked up at him as gratitude overwhelmed her. "I thought maybe being engaged would be enough. I really didn't expect I would have to be married."

"The terms of the will are explicit. Once the marriage certificate is signed, the inheritance will be completed. In the meantime, he let you have the key so you can have a look at the place."

She shook her head and tried to shake off the feeling she was in a dream. Even though she had known from the letter the inheritance all hinged on her being married, deep down she hadn't really thought it would happen.

"Bri."

He shortened her name and she liked the roll of the abbreviation in his deep voice.

"All I could think of was my family and what it would be like not to have known my own mother. And I knew you now had the opportunity to find out about your own birth mother." He shook his head, a rueful expression on his face. "You don't know me very well, but let me tell you, never have I made a decision so quickly in my life."

"I'm still not sure it's the right thing to do, but I guess we're sort of stuck with each other till we get this sorted."

Looking up into his face, she was taken aback by his expression. Something serious, something much deeper than a friendship was in his gaze and her heart pounded a warning.

She sat back in her seat, pulling away from the arm still loose around her shoulder. "Okay, it's time we made an agreement here. We can't risk doing it through the lawyer, so we'll have to draw up something and sign it together."

"Cross our hearts and hope to die? In blood." He grinned unapologetically. "Sorry, I have brothers."

"Talk about loosening up. Must be the Mediterranean air. Don't be flippant." She shook her head and grinned back at him. "I appreciate what you've done, but we do need some sort of agreement. For all you know, I might demand half your money when we annul the marriage."

"That's a good idea," he said, the grin still on his face. "You never know, I might want half your cottage in six months."

Brianna looked at him curiously. When he dropped the serious face, Tom had quite a sense of humour. Before she could reply, an elderly woman stood and pulled the bell rope and the bus stopped in the middle of a cobblestoned square in Cannetto.

"We're here," said Brianna. "Come on."

***

They stood on the crest of the hill on the northern side of the village. Tom had sought directions from the bus driver who had told them to follow the road through to the other side of the little village.

"It's magnificent." Brianna took a deep breath and stood staring out over the sea.

Mount Stombroli lay seven miles to the north across the Tyrrhenian Sea. Clouds of smoke hung over the volcanic island and contrasted with the deep blue sky and the azure waters of the sea. From the side of the road, the hill ran steeply down to a magnificent white beach.

"Oh, I do hope we can see the water from the cottage."

"Come on, let's find this place and then all your questions will be answered." Tom tugged at her hand and they walked up the steep hill.

"Are you sure he gave you the right directions?" Brianna asked stopping and pulling a water bottle from her bag after they had climbed for another ten minutes.

"Yes, I am sure. It should be around the next bend."

She skipped ahead of him and he smiled to himself. From a distance, she looked like a teenager with her long gangly legs and her dark braid flying in the breeze as her excitement at seeing her mother's house spurred her along.

A whitewashed villa sprawled down the hill at the end of the road. The vista of the sea formed a scenic backdrop to the waves breaking gently on the pebbled beach far below them.

"Is this it?" He strode down the hill and caught up to Brianna who stood at a locked wrought iron gate. Tom peered over the top of the intricately scrolled metal into a paved courtyard with a small fountain in the middle. Wind chimes tinkled and the soft sound of the cascading water greeted them from inside.

"This is it. La Casa Bianca." Tom held the key out. "The White House."

"But . . . but . . . it's not a cottage. It's a lot posher than I imagined. I thought it was going to be a wee cottage." Bianca's hand shook as she inserted the large key Mr. Antoniolli had given them. To Tom's surprise the gate opened noiselessly on the first turn of the key and they stepped through.

"Oh, my God. Look at this." Bianca turned to him, wide-eyed. "Is this really the right place? Is this my mother's place? Did the lawyer say it's really going to be mine?"

"Twenty questions again, Bri?" He couldn't help grinning at her delight and stood back as she whirled around and took off to the side of the building.

He followed her slowly, allowing her time to have her first look alone.

It wasn't a cottage. It was a small villa that was well cared for, and it was obvious from the pots of pink and red geraniums spilling down the sides of the wall overlooking the sea that someone still maintained it on a regular basis. The windows shone, and the pungent smell of thyme growing in the cracks between the cobblestones floated in the still air as it crushed beneath his feet.

Brianna stood at the wall overlooking the white pebbled beach far below, with her back to him, hands gripping the bricks tightly, her shoulders shaking. The unpredictability of this woman left him guessing most of the time. The emotions she showed freely confused him. He hesitated, unsure if she was laughing or crying this time, and then walked across and stood next to her. He breathed in deeply, as the heady aroma of the geraniums and herbs filled his senses and followed her gaze. Below the whitewashed brick edge of the balcony, a steep hill covered in yellow wildflowers led down to the shoreline. There was another small gate at the side of the balcony opening to a rough stone path that meandered along the cliff down to the water.

"I know I'm being emotional." She turned and smiled shakily up at him through her tears. "But it's so amazing. Pinch me, Tom. Tell me this is real. I'm not dreaming?"

He patted her on the arm. God, he'd run a mile when his sisters had gone through their teenage emotional stage and he'd didn't know how to react to Brianna. "Okay?"

She turned into him and he held his arms out. She buried her wet face in his chest, taking gulping sobs as he rubbed her back. Her whole body was shaking. This time there was no laughter. The loose hair from her braid tickled his nose, and as he turned his head to the side, he inhaled the sweet jasmine scent of her hair.

"I don't know if I can even go inside. I thought I could do this. I had childhood strange childhood. Even though I love Mum and Dad, and Phil, and Susie to pieces, I never truly belonged in the family. When I got the letter, the thought of Italy and a little cottage took over. But Tom—" She pulled back and he looked down into her red-blotched face—"this is my mother's house, my real flesh and blood mother who gave birth to me, and now I know she's dead and I'll never see her, but I feel like I've come home. This is where I belong."

Tom's eyes pricked at the mix of grief and happiness on her face.

"Are you going to be all right to meet your grandfather later? You don't have to do it all in one day."

"Yes," she said dragging in a deep breath. She touched his shirt, which was damp from her tears. "Thank you, you're a good man. Now come with me while I explore my mother's home, my new home."

The same large key opened the ornate metal screen door leading into the villa from the back courtyard. Like the outside of the house, the interior was clean and well maintained. Even though it was empty, it was not musty and had a welcoming feel. Tom followed Brianna as she walked slowly from room to room. The villa was spacious and the two bedrooms, small bathroom, and living area adjoining the tiny kitchen were bursting with colour. Pottery, rugs, and paintings in bold, bright colours contrasted with the stark white walls and the white tiled floors. Each room had an external door opening out to the balcony, which wrapped around the whole house.

Brianna was quiet as they looked around. She stopped in the living room and ran her hand along the back of the deep sofa and stood looking out over the water. Every room faced the sea. Comfortable chairs sat by the large windows and brightly covered shawls and throw rugs graced every piece of furniture. The afternoon sunlight streamed in onto the tiled floor. She slowly pulled open a cupboard door in one of the bedrooms and sighed softly.

"Oh my God. Look, Tom, all my mother's things are still here. It's like an Aladdin's cave."

She opened doors and cupboards until it overwhelmed her. Her throat clogged with tears and she decided to wait until she moved in before she examined the rest of the possessions her mother had left in the house.

"Come on, let's head back to Lipari," she said. "It's a bit much to take in all at once, and there have been enough tears for one day." She caught Tom's hand as he passed her the key to lock the door.

"Tom . . ."

He gazed down into her face, her eyes bright but clear of tears.

"Yes? What's wrong?"

"I've been thinking. Look, I'm still getting my head around all this. After we get married—" She stopped and giggled—"Shite, can you believe I said that? I really feel like I am dreaming."

"Yes?"

"You know you'll have to move in here with me. You said your aunt's apartment was too small. We'll have to keep up the appearance of being married so you can't go finding an apartment. But now I've seen it and felt it . . . there's no way I'm letting this opportunity go." She met and held his gaze. "Not because it's a lovely little villa perched on top of an island in the Mediterranean, but because it was my mother's." She grabbed both his hands and looked at him, her eyes wide. "What do you think, Tom? There are two bedrooms. There's the bus down to Lipari every day, although if it wasn't for the hills, the villages are close enough to walk between."

Tom's gut clenched. Her wide green eyes were bright with happiness. It made sense and he did need somewhere to live, and if they were going to go through with this marriage, they would have to make it appear real or it would be for nothing. But he wasn't sure, things were going way too fast for his liking, even though he'd told the lawyer they'd get married, he hadn't really expected it would happen.

"What do you think? Could you agree to live with me for a few months? Could you stand it?" She spoke fast and her words ran together. "I'll be busy writing my book, and I promise to leave you in peace and give you some space."

Looking down at her, a surge of affection rushed through him and he smiled.

"I think I could stand it, and I am very grateful for the offer." He reached across and wiped a single tear from her cheek with the pad of his thumb. "After all, you don't really know me."

"How about a simple agreement, sealed with a kiss." He bent his head and briefly pressed his mouth on her trembling lips. He pulled back as a surge of desire headed straight to his groin.

He turned away before she could glance down and see the effect of that single kiss.

"You lock up," he said gruffly. "I'll wait out

here. We'll go down to Lipari and you can meet my aunt."

She looked at him with a knowing glance, and he cursed inwardly as she turned to the door. It was obvious she knew why he'd turned away, even though he'd tried to change the subject.

It was a shame the island was so small. There was no way they could get a legal agreement drawn up and keep it quiet. They would have to draw up a gentlemen's agreement. It could jeopardise her inheritance if they got it done on the island. He'd surprised himself when he had told Mr. Antoniolli they had waited before they came to Italy to get married. There was nothing in it for him, but it would solve the problem of his matchmaking aunt. And that was almost payment enough for what he was about to do, for a perfect stranger.

Chapter Eight

Brianna's nerves got the better of her as they waited outside the Aunt Carmen's apartment. She paced up and down the narrow footpath as Tom rang the doorbell a second time.

"Maybe, she's not home?" she said hopefully.

"She's expecting us." Tom reached out and took her hand. "Come on, she might be down in the office." A surge of warmth shot up Brianna's arm at his touch as he pulled her along. She wasn't used to having a reaction like this when a man touched her casually.

He wasn't her usual type and she pushed her emotions aside and tried to think logically. She was obviously a bit fragile with all the family stuff happening.

That's all it was.

They walked down a narrow path at the side of the building and walked along a short wharf back to the office. An elderly woman in a bright pink dress had her arms around a woman sitting at the desk. As they entered the room, the younger woman stood and pointed at Tom.

"Sto lasciando questo lavoro"

She picked up her elegant leather bag and slung it over her shoulder and walked across to Brianna. Dressed in what appeared to be a designer suit and four inch heels, she towered over Brianna who was still dressed in her shorts, T-shirt, and sturdy walking boots.

"Pah, she looks like *ze* boy anyway. You will be sorry you didn't marry me. You could have had a real woman."

Brianna's heart plummeted and she looked from Tom to the elderly woman in confusion. Tom already had a girlfriend here? He hadn't even mentioned her.

At least the house was signed over, but they still had to go through with the marriage before it was final. And from his conversation earlier, she knew Tom was having second thoughts and now she knew why.

"Tom?"

"Don't worry, I'll explain later. Helena just quit her job." His face was flushed and she could see the pulse beating in his cheek. She pulled her hand out of his and turned away.

"Brianna, this is my Aunt Carmen."

The old woman enfolded her in a close hug and Brianna blinked to clear the tears pricking behind her eyelids

"I am very happy to meet you, Aunt Carmen.

May I call you that?" She rushed on, not sure what she was trying to prove, but it was a way to get Tom's intentions out in the open.

"Are you able to delay your trip? I would love you to stay for our wedding."

***

Tom sat in the work yard of the marina looking out across the small harbour, watching Matteo, the young labourer, sand down the hull of a hire boat. Apart from the recently departed secretary, there were no other employees.

"Shit," he muttered. "Double shit."

Aunt Carmen had spent the better part of the afternoon showing him through the office and the overflowing boxes that comprised her financial records. When he asked if she had a computer, she had simply shaken her head and pointed to the boxes and handwritten ledgers on the table. The record keeping of the business was in such a mess that it would take him weeks to sort it out. If he'd known how bad it was, he would never have bought the business. In fact, he probably would never have come to Italy. For a moment he wished he was back in his organised office at the university with his own apartment to go home to.

He'd had no idea that the business records were in such an archaic state. The information her accountant had sent over to him had seemed to indicate there was some sort of computer system in place. But no, it was all handwritten. He would buy a computer and hire a new secretary who would enter data until at least this year's records were in some sort of system.

"Shit," he said again.

That is if there were any records. There didn't appear to be any activity. It seemed the hire boat business had died along with Uncle Renzo last year. All he had was a couple of old boats and one workman. No tourist trade, no hire boats, no day trips.

His aunt had been delighted to meet Brianna and had agreed to delay her departure until after the wedding. He certainly didn't want to upset her with questions about the marina; he'd just have to get on with it the best he could.

God, he had so much on his mind.

The look on Brianna's face when Helena had been so rude to her was something he couldn't shake from his mind. He'd have to explain to her late he didn't even know the woman. She'd made it sound as though they'd practically been engaged.

How did every part of his life get so complicated in a few short days?

He looked down at the cell phone in his hand. There were a couple of calls he had to make. Or maybe he'd just call Nick? He stared at his phone wondering what the hell he was going to tell his family. They'd think he'd gone mad.

"Okay . . . deep breath. Which one?"

He shook his head. He was going bonkers sitting here talking to himself. Choosing the easy option, he punched in the speed dial for Nick.

After a long silence the international connection clicked through and he waited for Nick to pick up, hoping at the same time he wouldn't. He thought he was crazy and he knew his brother would give it to him. Perspiration trickled into his eyes, and he used the back of his hand to wipe his brow. He remembered how Brianna had soaked his shirt with her tears when she'd seen her mother's villa.

I'm doing the right thing.

"Tomas." Nick's voice replaced the buzzing ringtone. "You there, bro?" said Nick

"Hello, Nick, it's Tom."

"Yeah, I know, you mutt. I have caller ID. How's *la dolce vita*?"

"The what?"

"The sweet life. With all those gorgeous Italian girls Aunt Carmen has surely introduced you to already."

Tom looked out over the marina at the coloured sails fluttering in the breeze and the two small skiffs racing each other across the harbour. The hulls of the small craft slapped on top of the waves and the call of the spectators on the shore encouraged them to go faster.

"Great, all good. I got here in one piece and Aunt Carmen is as delightful as ever, although I have my work cut out with the business. Her accountant was less than honest in his outline of the financial system."

"It'll do you good to get some Italian sun and relax away from your computer for a change."

"Ah, Nick . . ."

"What's up?"

"Ah . . ."

"What's the matter? Is everything okay?"

Tom paused and a frisson of excitement tingled down his spine and he cleared his throat. "I rang to see if you and Lissy were settled in to your new jobs in Auckland . . . er . . . and to tell you I'm getting married tomorrow."

For a full minute, there was silence, and Tom looked at the screen thinking the connection had dropped and was about to press end and redial when Nick's voice roared through the phone.

"Are you taking the piss out of me? What do you mean you're getting married? And I thought I heard you say tomorrow!" Tom could hear Lissy in the background.

"Long story, Nick. It's all good. I'll send you an email when I get my internet connection all sorted. The service is unreliable over here. Do me a favour, tell Mama I have some news, and tell everyone I'll call in a couple of days. I'll try and get

Aunt Carmen to hold off ringing Mama, but I know what they're like. I didn't want her ringing before I got a chance to call. I'll talk to you in a few days. Okay?"

He spoke over Nick as his brother continued to protest. "*Ciao.* Give my love to Lissy."

His phone rang almost as soon as he disconnected the call.

"What the f—. All right, Lis . . . okay, I'll calm down." Nick's voice roared through the phone. "Tom, I swear if you don't tell me what's going on, I'll jump a plane and come there. What do you mean you're getting married? Are you kidding me?"

"Calm down. It's all above board. I'm helping out a friend out with a legal issue. She has to be married for an inheritance and I'm helping out, but keep that quiet. That's between you and me. According to the lawyer, there's already a bit of bad blood between the families and I don't want it to get around."

Nick's curse came down the phone, and Tom held it away, but the deep tones of his brother's voice came through even with the phone held away from his ear.

"What friend? You don't have any friends."

"Thanks, mate. I'll remember that one."

"Oh, Christ, Tom, you know what I mean. You don't have any friends in Italy."

"It's all right. We sealed an agreement this morning and it's only for a few months."

He closed his eyes as Nick continued questioning him and remembered the feel of Brianna's open lips beneath his as they had sealed the agreement. Her lips had been soft against his and had clung for a few seconds longer than he'd intended.

"Five minutes you've been away from home. Tom . . . you are such a soft touch . . . haven't you learned anything yet? You think you are going to get bloody married just to help out some stranger on the make? Mate, she saw you coming."

Hot anger burned up from his stomach. He was sick of being the responsible brother.

"Don't treat me like a fool." His voice was cold and it seemed to get through to his brother straightaway.

"Oh for God's sake. Be careful. Don't go getting yourself into anything messy."

Tom smiled to himself. "Don't worry, mate. It's not messy," he said as his temper cooled. "I'll call you in a couple of days, but first can you please tell Mama what's happening in case Aunt Carmen decides to ring her. She's going to witness the ceremony."

He ended the call and leaned back against the wall before glancing at the time on his phone. It was almost time to meet Brianna at the small café. He grinned to himself and shook his head. She was hopeless. Her cell phone charger had disappeared and she couldn't charge her phone so she was going to email the news of her inheritance to her family in Scotland from the public computer in the small café in the square. Only about the inheritance—she'd decided not to tell them about the marriage until it was all over. "The less family involved the better," she'd said.

It was shame he'd had to tell his family, but he knew Aunt Carmen wouldn't be able to keep a secret, and he couldn't tell her the truth in case it got back to the lawyer or Brianna's grandfather.

***

Brianna stood outside the café and watched Tom walk across the cobblestoned square toward her. Much to her surprise he was late. She'd finished emailing the family and knew there would be a flurry of emails in return when they found out she was in Italy, but she'd told them no details. It was now late in the afternoon and the village centre was deserted, the only sound the gushing of the water directed by Neptune in the fountain. She'd been waiting for Tom for over half an hour and was starting to wonder if he'd changed his mind. Ever since she'd met Aunt Carmen and the woman who was upset that she was marrying Tom, her mind had been in turmoil. And now she had to meet with her grandfather.

She squared her shoulders and bit down on her lip. This was going to be difficult.

Her grandfather. A flesh and blood relative.

It was so hard to believe. The strange old man in the lawyer's office had unnerved her and her stomach churned. Thank goodness Tom was coming also, so there could be no misunderstanding if her grandfather couldn't understand her English.

Tom stood beside one of the outside tables and waited for her to join him. She smiled at him when he pulled the chair out for her. He'd had his wee sulk on the plane when he'd thought she was psychoanalysing him, but the moodiness had left him since they'd arrived on the island.

The light breeze from the harbour blew his damp hair into disarray and she smiled. He was looking more relaxed every day. The formal suit he had worn to the lawyer's office this morning had been replaced by snug fitting jeans and a tight black T-shirt, and he looked like an Italian local with his dark hair and olive skin.

"You're looking very casual." She tipped her head to the side.

"I've been jet skiing. I've started on the list. One down, ten to go" A wide grin crossed his face. "Sorry I'm a bit late, but after I came back in Matteo wanted to show me the hire boats that need repairing. He wants to teach me how to do it and then we'll be able to hire them out again."

She shook her head, unable to picture it.

"Don't look so sceptical. I'm not totally a businessman. I can sand and fix a few little boats. And I can't face that office yet. And you know what? I've crossed two things off the list."

She smothered a laugh. Most of the boats in the harbour and dotted around the shoreline were not so little. "What's the second thing you've crossed off?"

"I haven't made a list since I got here."

Brianna sat back and looked at Tom and a funny feeling filled her chest. He was so damned attractive. If they didn't have all this hassle hanging over them, she would be tempted . . . But no, it would complicate matters too much. Which reminded her, they still had to come up with an agreement. She stifled a giggle—maybe they could put a sex clause in it.

They ordered their drinks and sat silent while the tourists disembarking from the afternoon ferry filled up the square.

"It is a beautiful place. And off the beaten tourist track. I'd never heard of Lipari until I received the letter from Mr . . . I mean *Signore* Antoniolli." Tom sipped his coffee and looked at her intently. "I have to get my head around this language if I'm going to stay here for a while."

"Do you think you'll stay for long?"

She shrugged. "Depends how it all pans out, I suppose. I know I've got the house, but it all rests on what happens with my...grandfather. I would really love to settle here for a while."

"Are you ready to meet him?"

"As much as I'll ever be, I suppose. I'm still trying to get used to having a real grandfather, like a blood relative." She sighed. "Just tell me a wee bit more about what the lawyer said."

"He said your grandfather was only happy for you to have the house once he assured him we were getting married on the island . . . and soon. I think he maybe doubtful about whether we are genuine or if we are just getting married for you to get your inheritance."

His face was serious and the doubt settled in Brianna's stomach.

"He seems to be an astute old thing. That's why I said we were getting married soon. It came out of nowhere."

"As long as you are sure you want to go through with this. What about your girlfriend?" She looked away from him and picked up the small teapot. Her hand shook as she poured her tea and waited for his answer. She'd waited for him to explain what that was all about, but he obviously wasn't going to mention it.

"Are you having second thoughts?" asked Tom.

She looked up and was surprised by the frown crinkling his forehead as though he would be disappointed if she changed her mind.

He was probably hoping she would.

"No. I'm worried about the huge favour you are doing for me. I can't understand why, especially when it's upset your girlfriend. Did you meet her in Australia?"

Tom looked at her and shook his head as he ran his hand though his hair in a frustrated gesture which was becoming quite familiar to her

"I don't have a girlfriend. She's Aunt Carmen's friend's daughter and for some reason she was expecting to get a job and a husband out of my visit. My aunt and her mother had obviously given here some expectations."

Tom reached over and took her hand and the usual heat rushed in.

"Honestly, I met her for the first time when I arrived at Aunt Carmen's after I dropped you at the hotel the other night." He pulled out his phone and checked the time. "It's almost time to meet him. Are you ready?"

Brianna jumped up and walked around the table. She stood behind Tom and draped her arms around his neck before bending down and kissing his cheek, letting her lips linger on his freshly shaved skin.

"Okay, even if I can't understand why, I

guess we need to make this look genuine if we're going to go through with it." With a deep breath she inhaled the citrus tang of his aftershave and a spark of desire ran down her spine as he looked back at her. This tug of attraction hit her at the strangest times, and she decided to put it down to her overcharged emotions. That's what it was. It was plain relief, not attraction. And he *was* a good-looking guy, so that was a bonus. She pulled back from him and tugged at his hand. "Come on then, we'd better get going."

"There's one more thing you need to know before we go," he said slowly as he stood.

She looked up at him, the tone of his voice worrying her.

"Oh God, what now?" She pulled her braid over her shoulder and twirled the loose hair at the end through her fingers.

"Apparently, there is some bad blood between our families."

"Well, that's nothing we can't sort out," she said. "Family feuds have nothing to do with us. It's just as well you're here to translate for me. If he doesn't speak English, I'll keep looking at you lovingly while you speak for me." She smiled and was pleased when he continued to hold her hand firmly in his as they made their way across the square back to the office of Bruni and Antoniolli.

Tom pushed open the door to the lawyer's

office and the secretary gestured for them to take a seat. It was a short time before they were ushered into Signore Antoniolli's office. Her grandfather was standing straight and tall, next to the lawyer.

Brianna looked up into his unsmiling face. His demeanour had changed since this morning's meeting when he had rushed out of the office, and her heart rate picked up. She forced a pleasant smile onto her face, determined not to let her nervousness show.

"*Buongiorno,*" said Tom holding out his hand. Her grandfather nodded and ignored Tom's proffered handshake.

Mr. Antoniolli directed them all to a seat before leaving the three of them alone in his office. They sat together in the small office until the silence became uncomfortable. Brianna gripped Tom's hand as her grandfather looked from one to the other. Eventually, he locked a wary gaze on Tom's face and spoke for a few moments.

Tom leaned over to Brianna after he replied to the old man. "He said he is happy to meet with us. He has heard the wedding is to be next week and asks if he may come."

"Well, I suppose that will be okay." Brianna's voice shook and Tom looked at her with concern on his face.

"You're sure you're okay with that?"

"Yes, as long as he doesn't look like he's at

a funeral rather than a wedding."

Tom turned to her grandfather and spoke briefly. The old man nodded and ran a shaking hand over his face. Tom translated for Brianna.

"I told him we'd let him know as soon as we have the documents sorted and book the ceremony."

"Tom . . ." Brianna tugged at his sleeve. "Ask him what I should call him?"

The old man turned to her, after Tom asked him and nodded. "*Nonno*." His voice was stern and his face was expressionless.

"Please ask him what his problem is." She didn't care what the answer was. She wanted everything out in the open, except the bit about the wedding being a sham, she thought.

A lengthy conversation ensued, and she watched the expressions play across Tom's face. She leaned into him when he placed his arm affectionately around her shoulders.

The old man stood and looked across at Brianna, blinking his faded eyes. Tears pricked at her eyes as she held his gaze and she didn't brush them away. She moved away from Tom's embrace and walked over to the old man, and took his hand. Reaching up, she brushed a soft kiss across the papery skin of his cheek.

"*Nonno,*" she said. He gripped her hand firmly, before he turned away and opened the door .

"Well?" She turned back to Tom as her

grandfather left the room. He held his arms out to her and leaned into him, appreciating his understanding of the emotion coursing through her

"Your mother left the island suddenly and didn't come back for a long time. Apparently, she left with no explanation and they never knew she'd had a baby. He is still unsure if you are really his granddaughter, but he'll accept what the lawyers say while he makes more enquiries. He's also a bit suspicious about the wedding, and he wants to make sure we really go through with it. He wants to know why we waited until we came to Lipari to get married, and I had to do a bit of quick thinking. He's suspicious the whole thing is a scam."

Tom looked guilty and a wave of compassion swept over Brianna. "I'm sorry, Tom. Are you sure you want to go through with this?"

Brianna's heart almost stopped as he frowned. He looked at her for a few minutes and indecision crossed his face. She was sure he was about to change his mind. She caught her breath.

"If you've changed your mind, tell me. And tell me now. I am not going to risk this. I won't lose the chance to get to know my mother. Even though she's dead, I can still find out about her life and I can live where she lived."

"This whole deception has got out of hand. It's starting to involve too many other people." His voice was firm. "It's not just about an inheritance any more. People are going to get hurt. And we're lying."

"So what are you trying to say?" The panic built in her chest and she fought the disappointment that was clawing through her chest. "Are you trying to tell me you've changed your mind?"

"No, I gave you my word. I've made a commitment and I won't go back on it. But I think we need to draw up an agreement before we go through with it."

Brianna pushed away the confusion filling her. She had a lot of things to get her head around, including the feelings she was starting to have for Tom, but in the meantime she had a wedding to plan, whether he believed it or not.

Chapter Nine

Tom received some appreciative glances as he pushed his way through the throngs of casually dressed tourists crowding the morning market next to the harbour. He pulled at the collar of his shirt. It was the first time he'd worn a suit since arriving in Italy, and it was constricting his neck after T-shirts all week. He strode up the road past the houses that seemed to be glued to the steep hillside overlooking the azure sea. Terraced gardens with grape, olive, and lemon trees and various vegetables provided a brilliant foreground to the intense blue of the mid-morning sky. Scarlet geraniums in window boxes and pots spilled down the front of the houses and sweet fragrances hung in the still, hot air.

He paused at the entry of the small hotel at the top of the hill and wiped the perspiration from his face before pushing open the front door. The reception area was deserted, manned by a huge ginger cat draped along the counter. It swiped a lazy paw at him as he walked past the office. Tom stood next to the desk for five minutes before glancing at his watch. He tapped his fingers on the counter.

Come on, Brianna, we're going to be late.

God, he didn't even know which room she

was in. Leaning over the cat, he looked at the large book on the desk, scanning down the room numbers. Number six. *Ballantyne*. The name stood out in elegant copperplate in the old-fashioned reservations book.

He climbed the stairs to the first floor and walked along until he reached her room at the end of the corridor. After tapping on the door, he crossed to the window that overlooked the square below, and he stood gazing down at the open-air market while he waited for her to open the door. After another five minutes had passed, he knocked again and a harried voice called through the door.

"All right, already . . . hold ye horses. I'm bloody coming."

Sweet. A ladylike bride.

He hadn't planned on a wife, let alone one whose language could get quite colourful at times. Five more minutes passed and he glanced at his watch. He eased himself into the cane chair by the window and waited patiently. Noticing a speck of dirt on his shoes, he pulled out his handkerchief and polished it off. Satisfied they were back to their glossy shine, he looked up and a pair of long bare legs filled his sight. He raised his eyes to the woman standing in front of the open door.

A vision in white confronted him. Brianna's olive skin accentuated the virginal white of the tight, short dress moulded to her figure like a second skin. Her feet were clad in a pair of barely there gold sandals, and her toenails were painted a soft pink. For the first time since he'd met her, her hair was loose and a torrent of black curls cascaded around her shoulders, one side pinned back by a small spray of red and yellow wildflowers.

His stomach contracted as though he'd been punched in the gut, and a frisson of desire shot straight to his groin.

"You're ready then?"

"Yes, I'm ready…I think." She smiled a shaky smile and reached over to tug the sleeve of his suit coat. "But don't you think you'll be too warm in a jacket?"

"It's a formal occasion. I thought a well-dressed groom was called for."

She reached up and brushed her lips across his cheek. "I'm sorry." She pulled back and looked at him. "I was only teasing, but you do realise how much I appreciate this?" A frown wrinkled her forehead. "God, how many men would meet someone on a plane and then marry them within the week?" She shook her head and looked at him in disbelief. "It's like a fairy-tale. I can't believe it. My mother's cottage turns out to be a villa. I have a real grandfather, even though he doesn't believe it yet. I really am starting to wonder about this. I always act without thinking, I know that."

Tom looked down at his watch and feigned

displeasure to divert his attention from the beautiful woman in front of him. She was not the flighty girl he'd felt sorry for last week. The braids and the casual shorts had disappeared. This was a woman oozing sex appeal and his libido appreciated it. And now she was the one having second thoughts.

"Unless we leave straight away, there's not going to be a wedding." He reached into his pocket and withdrew a handwritten piece of paper. Even though he'd typed the agreement in his laptop, there hadn't been a printer anywhere in the marina and he'd had to resort to handwriting. "So we'd better talk this over and decide if we are going to sign this or if we call it quits now." Brianna turned to pull the door closed and he gulped. Tanned smooth skin disappeared into a plunging deep V at the base of her back, and his fingers itched to run down her spine. He shoved his hands in his pockets and walked in front of her along the corridor to the narrow staircase. She stopped at the top of the stairs and sat down on the top step.

"Show me." She took the paper from his hands and quickly read the words. "Oh God, I don't know. Am I crazy?" Brianna looked up at him as he sat down next to her on the wooden step. "On second thought, don't answer that. I am. I know I'm crazy. I should never have suggested this in the first place." Her bare shoulder pressed against his and he ignored the jolt of heat rocketing through his body.

"Oh shit, Tom, I just thought. We haven't got rings. So that solves it. We can't go ahead with it."

"Yes, we have," he said, patting his pocket. "I've got a ring for each of us." He leaned over and put his arm around her, and as she leaned into him, her hair tickled his nose. "If you are going to change your mind, you have about two minutes to decide."

"What do you think?" She turned to him and he looked down at her. Her eyes were wide and full of trust.

She didn't really need to know what he was thinking at the moment because it had nothing to do with getting married and making the right decision. He was fighting the temptation to push her back into the carpeted hallway, put his lips on hers, and run his fingers along her bare shoulders.

But that wouldn't solve anything. It would only make matters worse. He removed his arm and cleared his throat, trying to regain his composure.

"I know," she said. "Let's make a list. Have you got a pen?"

Tom pulled a pen from the pocket inside his jacket. "What sort of list?"

"Of course you've got a pen. Who else would carry a pen to their wedding?" Brianna burst out laughing and he grinned back at her. "Okay. Pros and cons. And then if that doesn't work we'll vote."

He shook his head. "We can't vote with two. It wouldn't be fair to the loser."

"Shit, shit, shit." Brianna handed him back the agreement, leaned forward and put her elbows on her knees, and dropped her chin into her hands. "I honestly don't know what to do. It really isn't the right thing, is it?"

"Depends what we both want out of it. We're both going into it with our eyes open." Her uncertainty was hard to watch and he wanted to see her smile.

"We haven't even got time to make a list," she said.

"I know how to decide," he said keeping his voice serious.

He pushed himself to his feet and stepped down two of the stairs so his face was level with hers and then reached down and lifted one of her hands. He let go and lifted his other hand and held it in front of her.

"Rock, paper, scissors? Winner decides."

"Okay."

"Ready?" he said. She nodded.

"One, two, three . . . four!"

Tom laughed at both their palms extend flat in front of them. "Uh oh. A tie. What now?" he said. "Best of three?"

Brianna held her hand up to him and when

he held it, she pulled herself to her feet."

"No, no more time for games." She turned to him, her eyes alight with laughter. "Give me the pen and paper. You convinced me. Hurry up or we'll be late." They both signed the agreement and Tom put the piece of paper back in his pocket.

"Come on, then. You're getting to know me. I hate being late, and I'm not going to be late for my own wedding."

***

It was cooler in the dim foyer of the town hall and the three guests waited quietly. Brianna was surprised to see an elderly lady, obviously Tom's aunt, chatting to *Signore* Antoniolli. It was a small town so of course they'd know each other.

Her grandfather stood to the side, and looked across at her without a glimmer of a smile on his face, his beetling brows almost meeting. She looked away, and Tom, God love him, took her hand and squeezed it. His wedding, he'd said. Well, it was her day, too, and if she followed her heart and remained true to herself, it would be her only wedding. Once they annulled the marriage, there was no way she was ever going to marry again, so she might as well make the most of this one.

Tom led her to the celebrant, and Brianna felt like she was distanced from the whole proceeding. Here she was getting married in an Italian town hall, surrounded by strangers, and not understanding a word of it. Nervousness settled deep in her chest like an ache.

She swallowed, but the tightness rose up into her throat. Determined not to cry, she bit down on the side of her cheek so hard she tasted blood. But she failed and the urge to burst into tears got stronger. Tom elbowed her and she looked across at him, tears threatening to spill over onto her cheeks. She shook her head and he elbowed her again and inclined his head to the celebrant who was standing there with an expectant look on his face

Even though the language was musical and pleasant to listen to, she'd stopped paying attention when her nerves had taken hold, and she had no idea what the man was saying. After a few moments, Tom leaned across to her. "He's waiting for you to say you will take me as your husband."

Her nervousness disappeared as she looked up into Tom's deep blue eyes. The sexy crinkles around his eyes deepened as he smiled down at her. He'd drilled the words into her memory and she had practised it over and over.

"Err . . . *i sarà.*"

Aunt Carmen clapped and her grandfather nodded when the celebrant put their hands together and spoke solemnly.

"Si può baciare la sposa."

All thoughts of tears drifted away as Tom took her face between his hands and leaned his head toward hers. She held that sexy blue gaze with her own. He closed the distance between them. Desire rocked through her and her trembling legs threatened to give way. All she could think about was running her hands up underneath his shirt and touching his bare skin.

"Pay attention," Tom murmured against her mouth.

She opened her mouth to assure him that she was, and he kissed her, forestalling any protest from her.

Brianna sighed against his lips and looped her arms around his neck pulling him closer. Tom deepened the kiss and shivers skittered across her skin as he explored her mouth. She stiffened when he put his hand on her bare back to draw a lazy circle on her skin and his lips slid from her mouth to her cheek. Goose bumps rose on her arms. It was as if he'd read her mind. She'd been thinking about touching his skin and now his fingers were plating on her back.

He pulled back slowly and locked his gaze with hers. "Convincing enough?" he whispered. "Now you have your villa, Mrs. Richards."

The warmth tingling through her body disappeared as if a bucket of cold water had been thrown over her. For a brief minute she'd closed her eyes and pretended it was for real. Now she shivered, her body as cold as his voice.

Blinking, she looked around at the small group surrounding them. Tom kept a tight hold of her hand as a chorus of congratulations washed over them. His aunt chattered away to him in Italian and he pulled Brianna forward.

"*Zia*, this is Brianna, my wife."

Aunt Carmen kissed her soundly on both cheeks and gripped her hands.

Brianna looked across at her grandfather. A slight smile played about his mouth and he held her gaze and extended his old wrinkled hand to her. She took it and closed her eyes. She could smell garlic and hair cream on him, but didn't pull away as dry papery lips brushed her cheek. Unbidden tears filled her eyes, but before she could speak the old man turned away from her to Tom and shook his hand solemnly.

"*Più tardi,*" he said before tipping his hat and walking out of the room. She remembered the words from the lawyer's office yesterday.

Later.

"A meal, *si*?" Aunt Carmen glared at the back of the old man as he walked out of the door. "Pah, he has always been a stubborn old man."

Her expression changed to a beam when she turned to face them. "But it is your wedding and the rest of us will be so happy for you." She came over to Brianna and enfolded her in a close hug. "My sister would never forgive me if I did not make a fuss of you on your wedding day." She lifted her hands and placed gentle hands on each side of Brianna's face. Welcome to the family, *cara ragazza"*

Signore Antoniolli nodded and Brianna found herself swept out the door and into the hot sunshine. Aunt Carmen and the lawyer chattered non-stop as they crossed the square, and Tom still held her hand tightly. She looked at him. For someone who was playing a role, he was doing it pretty well.

"You can let go now, if you want."

He dropped her hand and she looked down at her hand as the sunlight glinted on her wedding ring.

"Jesus, Mary, and Joseph," she muttered under her breath. "What in the bloody hell have I done?"

Confusion overwhelmed her, and Tom cupped his hand beneath her elbow as they reached the restaurant. "Are you all right?"

"Yes, yes, I'm fine. It's just a bit hot." She grabbed a menu from the counter and fanned herself as they made their way through to the courtyard in the centre of the small restaurant. The waiter fussed around and seated the two women, and then poured them a glass of iced water. Aunt Carmen reached over and squeezed her hand. Her face had been wreathed in smiles since Brianna's grandfather had left them.

Brianna looked down at the small cake in the centre of the table as she sipped her drink. It was decorated with sugared flower petals, and had a plastic bride and groom stuck in the middle. She wondered who'd ordered it.

There was so much to process; it was as though she was in a dream. A week ago, she'd known none of these people, and now here she was sitting with a husband, his aunt, and the lawyer who had sent her that fateful letter.

Heat filled her cheeks and her hand shook as she fanned herself with the cardboard menu. "More water, please," she whispered.

Tom held her against him and placed the glass of water to her lips. She sipped gratefully and the faintness receded as fast as it had come.

"Sorry. I've been on a bit of an emotional roller coaster ever since I got that letter and it all just hit me."

Tom squeezed her hand, and kept his other arm around her bare shoulders while Aunt Carmen and *Signore* Antoniolli looked on affectionately

"You know, we didn't think this through very well," she whispered. "They're going to expect us to spend the night together."

"Brianna, my dear." He smiled and pushed the loose curls back from her forehead, before he whispered in her ear. "Don't worry. We don't have to please anyone except ourselves now that the marriage certificate is signed. Your mother's house is all yours and we have to keep a facade up for a few months until we get an annulment. It's as easy as that."

Gratitude overwhelmed her and for a moment she couldn't speak.

"Oh God, what a day. We did it." All she'd worried about was herself. What about Tom? How the hell had he got himself mixed up in her problems? She would be eternally grateful to him, but she hadn't given him much thought.

She grinned at him and reached over and straightened his suit jacket. "At least you got to wear your suit before it got packed away. A wedding wasn't on your list."

"What list? Do I look like a man who needs a list?"

She looked him up and down from his polished shoes to his crisp white shirt and straight tie and nodded with a grin.

"Aye, my man. You surely do."

"Well, I might now, but wait till you see Tom the boatman. He's the new happy-go-lucky, don't give a damn man."

She burst out laughing and grabbed his arm.

"I will be forever grateful, you know. Now, what can I do to help you out? How on earth can I ever repay you?"

"What do you know about boats?" he asked with a smile.

The meal continued into the afternoon, and Brianna ended up in her usual giggles when Signore Antoniolli decided to teach her some basic Italian. With the assistance of Tom's Italian and Aunt Carmen's English she learned several new phrases. Her working knowledge of the language now included more than *casa*, *vivace,* and *avocatto.*

Signore Antoniolli stood and raised his glass. *"Per cent'anni."*

Aunt Carmen nodded. "For one hundred years," she repeated in English.

"They are wishing us a happy marriage for one hundred years," Tom said.

Eventually, it became too warm to stay outdoors as the sun rose high in the sky above the open courtyard. Signore Antoniolli picked up his hat and cane, and swept into a deep bow before he took Brianna's hand in his.

"Congratulazioni, mia cara."

Aunt Carmen grabbed both Tom and Brianna in a close hug and then Signore Antoniolli escorted her out of the courtyard and down the cobblestoned street.

Tom sat back and sipped his wine and looked at Brianna, his face inscrutable.

Brianna sat back as well and looked across

at him. "Well?"

"Well what?"

"What now?"

"I guess we have to decide where we are going to spend our wedding night." Tom put his wine glass down and frowned. "Are you too tired to get your things from the hotel and move up to the villa this afternoon, or do you want me to get another room at your hotel to keep appearances up?"

"You sure can't go back to your aunt's place." Brianna looked across at him and a wave of true affection swept over her. She grabbed both his hands in hers and turned his left hand over and looked down at his wedding ring.

"How did you get the rings so quickly?"

"Comes from being organised," he said with a smile. "And having contacts. Matteo's father owns the jewellery shop across the square."

"It's a beautiful ring and entirely appropriate. Thank you." She held her hand in front of her and the bright sunlight glinted off the Celtic love knots on the gold ring. "I'm not too tired and we have plenty of time left this afternoon to move into the villa. Come on, we'll go back to the hotel. I'll get changed and then we can spend the night at the house and decide how we are going to play this. I am worried my grandfather is still a wee bit suspicious. He didn't crack a smile the whole time he was there."

Tom stood and pulled her gently to her feet, and rested his chin on the top of her head.

"Did I tell you what a beautiful bride you are?"

"Thank you, but you don't have to. It's not as if I'm a real bride."

"But you are still a very beautiful bride."

Embarrassed by his words, she tried to play it down. He was so hard to figure out and she was not going to get sucked in by him.

"A bit different to my usual look, you mean," she said briskly. "Come on. It's time to go."

***

Later that afternoon, Tom stood on the balcony at the side of the villa. It was a beautiful home and full of vibrant colours. The atmosphere in the house suited Brianna's personality, and he wondered if she took after her mother. He had never met anyone so full of the joy of life and so open.

Shit. He cursed under his breath. *Pull back, mate.*

Although after a few days in Italy, he was pretty comfortable with the way things were shaping up. He stood on the balcony watching the sea darken as the sun disappeared. Grey waves were whipped up by the early evening breeze and the chill of the evening settled. He shivered and turned to go inside where Brianna was unpacking.

If it could be called unpacking.

He stood and watched, trying not to laugh. Her suitcase had exploded in the middle of the tiled floor of the living area.

"How did you manage to fit all of that into one bag?" he asked with a grin. Clothes and books, folders and papers, and a tangle of computer cables surrounded her on the floor. There was even a small printer peeking out from underneath a pile of underwear.

She looked up at him and laughed. "Told you I wasn't organised. Now you'll get to see it."

He kneeled down next to her on the tiled floor. "Can I help?

"It's okay, I'll tidy it up. I'm just looking for my PJs." She lowered her lashes. "Do I need them?" She paused and then looked up and held his gaze. "We haven't discussed the finer details of our agreement. After all, it is our wedding night."

Tom's stomach lurched and his mouth went dry. His heart pounded a slow heavy beat and the blood pumped through his limbs. He stood there looking at her until Brianna pushed herself to her feet and walked over to him, and placed her hands on his shoulders. She reached up and ran a butterfly kiss across his lips and he closed his eyes as the smell of jasmine from her loose hair assailed his senses.

"I know what we discussed, but our

agreement was only sealed with a kiss, remember?" she said softly. "Keep the legal mumbo jumbo filed away for when we finish the marriage."

She looked earnestly up into his face and the tip of her small pink tongue touched her top lip.

Leaning over close to him, her voice was hesitant, but then her tongue touched his lips in invitation. "Will you come to bed with me, Tom?"

Tom's world tilted on its axis, but he held her shoulders and stepped back, putting some space between them. He bit down on the anger building in his chest as he tried to find the right words to say without losing his temper and hurting her feelings. He knew it was only gratitude on her part. No matter how much he wanted her, he didn't sleep with anyone out of gratitude. He shook his head slowly.

"I don't sleep with anyone because they think they owe me for a favour."

"No . . . listen to me, Tom. Hear me out. Looking at you makes me feel, well, you should . . . you should know. We're adults, and unless I'm reading you the wrong way, you're attracted to me as well. So we might as well share a bed and have some fun while we're here together." She put her hands on his shoulders and stood on tiptoes. "I know this isn't for real, and I know neither of us wants that, but it's the least I can do."

It was the second time she'd said that.

Tom lifted her hands from his shoulders and placed them by her side and walked across to the window. He was tempted to take her in his arms and kiss her, but he was determined to walk away from the temptation. It wasn't the way he wanted it to happen. Not because she felt she owed him something for a marriage certificate. If indeed it ever happened.

She looked up at him, and those green eyes that had been brimming with tears over the past week were alight with laughter, and her lips parted as she stared at him.

"I don't expect sexual favours because I have helped you out, Brianna."

She burst out laughing.

"Oh, God, Tom. You're so uptight. Look, I'll make you another deal. You helped me out. I'm more than happy for you to be my 'bidie-in,' and I'll help you get over your hang-ups."

"My what?"

"Oh, you know what I mean," she said with a dismissive wave of her hand.

"No, Miss Psychologist, I don't know what you mean. And how would you know if I have sexual hang-ups? You've known me less than a week and you don't know anything about me. And I don't know anything about you. That's the reason we need to take this slow." He glared at her. "If we take it anywhere at all."

"I think we need to make an agreement. For all I know you're after half my villa. We should have done that before. I'm surprised you didn't insist on it, *Mr. Organised*."

"A legal agreement?"

"Yes, a legal agreement. Just in case I'm after your marina."

He laughed. "For what it's worth."

She turned away from him and her face was hidden in the shadows. "Just in case you think I might be on the make, we need to make an agreement. Between you and me, seeing we can't involve the lawyers. I'll go and get my laptop and you can type it up."

"No, thank you. We're not going to do that while we're both angry." Tom forced his anger down. "We'll sort out an agreement in the morning and we'll email it to our own lawyers. Okay?"

"Alright, then. I'm going to bed."

"Where shall I sleep?"

"I've put my stuff in the room near the bathroom," she said, her back still turned to him. "You can have the other one or the lounge. I don't give a shit."

"Brianna?"

She turned slowly and her face was closed, her Scottish burr clipped.

"What?"

"You are a very beautiful woman, but I

don't think gratitude is a good basis for a sexual relationship."

"No matter, I've changed my mind anyway. We can live here together as strangers and when your visit's up, you can go on your merry way with all your finances intact. Our agreement will make sure you don't try to get half shares in *my* villa. After all, you don't trust me. Why should I trust you?"

She slammed the teapot into the sink. "Now, I'm going to bed." She stomped across the living room into the bedroom, and slammed the door.

"I do trust you," he said quietly.

"Whatever," came the muffled reply through the closed door.

Chapter Ten

The soughing of the waves washing back over the pebbly beach below the villa woke Tom before sunrise. His chest was heavy as he remembered the argument with Brianna.

God, he was so damn attracted to her and knew he'd hurt her feelings. It had taken him ages to get to sleep. Logic told him it was way too soon to get involved with her. He was still not ready to go down that path, no matter how much she tempted him.

He tended to avoided situations like this—he hated conflict and messy emotions. Give him a financial problem to nut out any day. When you didn't depend on anyone else you didn't have to deal with all the emotional crap that came with it. He much preferred his life to be organized and predictable.

So what the hell was he doing? He'd been happy with the agreement as it stood, and then Brianna had to go and ruin it all last night. He hated not being in control.

Friends with benefits was not the way he operated.

He dozed back off and woke a while later

when the bed creaked and moved. He rolled over to his side. Or rather, he attempted to roll over. A weight on his chest and legs prevented him from moving and he opened his eyes slowly. Tom groaned and immediately closed them. He kept them squeezed shut, hoping he was still asleep and this was a dream, but a little giggle and a tickle of hair on his bare chest convinced him he was awake and his wife of less than twenty-four hours was straddling his bare legs.

Brianna was perched on his thighs with her knees resting on each side of him on the crisp white sheets. "Open your eyes. I know you're awake.

Tom obeyed reluctantly. Her black curls tumbled in wild disarray over her bare shoulders and skimmed the edge of the sheet she clutched over her loose T-shirt.

"Brianna, what . . . what the hell do you think are you doing? Stay there any longer and I won't be responsible for what happens." He closed his eyes, covered them with one hand and waited for her to leave.

No such luck. Or more to the point, he was about to get lucky.

"I'm apologising to you."

"Apologising?"

"Yes, I was a right cow last night."

He opened his eyes again and tried to pull the other side of the sheet up over his bare stomach.

"Don't say a word," she whispered.

He opened his mouth to speak. She leaned forward and placed her fingers over his mouth.

"Now I want your full attention for a wee while, and if I start babbling tell me to put a sock in it."

Tom was in no state to think about socks or anything else. His brain had joined the lower half of his anatomy. He nodded without opening his eyes, fighting between the fading desire for her to leave and the need to grab her and roll on top of her.

"That's good. Don't say a word, hear me out. I was a bitch last night. I was upset, but when I thought about it, I know I was unfair to you. You're the one doing the favour and it was mean of me to say I didn't trust you." She paused to take a breath. "Open your eyes, so I can see what you're thinking."

Tom obeyed and lay there looking up at her, calling on his sheer strength of will to kill the desire that was running rampant through his blood.

He failed.

"We're both adults. If I insulted you by offering to sleep with you again last night, I'm sorry, but the truth is I wanted you. Every time I looked at you yesterday, all I could think about was taking that suit off you and peeling your white shirt off. But I went about it the wrong way last night and then that stupid phone call upset me and—"

"You're babbling. Now listen to me." Tom swallowed as her fingers traced circles on his bare chest. "We've only known each other a few days, and we've landed ourselves in a situation. You know I trust you. If I didn't, I would never have offered to marry you. I don't want to take advantage of you and the situation."

She smiled at him and wriggled on his legs and he tried to keep his eyes away from the gentle swell of her breasts beneath her T-shirt.

"I don't think it would be taking advantage of me and isn't that what counts? It's more than gratitude. More like friends with benefits."

He sighed when she repeated the words that had been in his head a couple of minutes ago.

"We are friends, aren't we, Tom?" She lowered her voice to a sexy purr and the Scottish lilt in her voice sent desire rocketing through his entire body.

"Brianna, whatever we are . . . can we talk about it later?" The heat was moving between his face, his neck and he couldn't think straight.

"Now don't go getting in a *fankle*," she said.

"A what?"

"You know a tizzy, a right state."

"Ah, but Brianna, I'm already in a right state and . . . er . . . I don't have any clothes on." He tried to grab the sheet, which was crossed over her legs. Instead, she lifted the sheet and peeked underneath it. "Well, well, Tomas . . ." she said with a cheeky smile.

She leaned forward and her hair brushed his chest. She picked up his hand and moved it behind his head, closing his fingers around the black pine bed posts.

"What are you doing?"

"I'm saying sorry, seeing you don't want me to say thank you. It's the morning after our wedding. We had a civilised agreement which—" she said leaning forward and brushing his lips with hers "—we sealed with a kiss. I think we need to change the agreement. After all, we're both old enough to know what we want, aren't we?"

She sat back and lifted the sheet, peeked underneath again, and smiled down at him.

"Don't we, Tom?"

Tom couldn't move. The weight of her pressed onto his thighs, and he was sure he was about to lose it. He usually hated not being in control, but this situation was getting more enjoyable by the minute.

"I have a plan," she said and looked across at the bed table. Tom followed her quick glance and almost choked when he saw a row of foil packets placed in a neat line along the edge of the table. They hadn't been there the night before.

"Now . . . I'm *sorra* for losing my temper last night." Her Scottish burr became more pronounced as she spoke and he narrowed his eyes when the pink flush deepened high on her olive cheeks. He held her gaze and noticed her lips trembling slightly. Warmth filled his chest as he understood what she was playing at.

It's all an act.

She was as nervous as a virgin bride, scared he would reject what she was offering.

"Okay, tell me your plan." At least he could control his voice. He made a mammoth effort to sound calm and to ignore the woman who was trying her best to tempt him. As if reading his mind, she wriggled to get more comfortable and his calm flew out the window.

"First things, first," she said and reached over for one of the foil packets. "Are you happy for me to continue?"

"Yes," he managed to choke out.

"And we are going to rework our deal?"

Tom gulped and nodded as she lay beside him.

With a deep groan, he rolled over to face her. Cheeky eyes full of mirth met his. She opened her mouth to speak, but he pressed his lips against hers.

"No words," he murmured against her mouth. "Now, I'll show you *my* plan. Step one."

"I like your style," she murmured as he took the packet from her.

***

Tom woke much later in the morning. The sun had passed over to the other side of the villa and the room was dim. Instead of worry in his chest and a sexy weight on his legs waking him, Brianna's warm even breath puffed against his lips. Her hair tickled his nose and he opened his eyes as one of his favourite songs flitted through his thoughts.

I could stay lost in this moment forever.

He stroked his hand down her cheek and pushed her hair away from her face back onto the pillow. She sighed in her sleep and snuggled into him. His body responded, and he leaned closer to nuzzle his lips into her cheek.

"It's time we were up," he murmured.

A rhythmic creaking sound drifted in through the open window, and he lifted his head away from her hair and turned to the sound. The grating of a key in the metal gate on the back balcony followed. He shook Brianna's shoulder when he heard a voice call out, *"Allo? Allo?"*

"Brianna," he whispered. "There's somebody in the kitchen."

"What?" She sat up and smiled at him, her expression relaxed and contented.

"There's somebody in the kitchen." His words were confirmed by the running of water and the clanging of dishes in the sink. Then a quavering female voice burst into song.

"Bells will ring ting-a-ling-a-ling, Ting-a-ling-a-ling and you'll sing, "Vita bella"

Hearts will play tippy-tippy-tay

Tippy-tippy-tay like a gay tarantella"

"What's that noise? Who's in my house?" Brianna clutched the sheet, wrapping it around her as she climbed out of bed. She marched to the door, followed closely by Tom who grabbed his jeans from the floor and pulled them on. He put his hands on Brianna's shoulder and stepped past her. A short elderly woman with rosy cheeks and grey hair pulled tight into a bun grinned at them across the living room. She clapped her hands delightedly and laughed.

"Oh, so happy for you . . . so, so happy!"

"Ah, excuse me," said Brianna. "Who are you and where did you get the key to . . . er . . . my house?"

The woman shuffled across the tiles and met them at the doorway. She grabbed Brianna and kissed her on both cheeks, and Tom reached for the sheet when it started to slip.

"Oh, you are so like your mama." Tears welled in the woman's eyes.

"You *knew* my mother?"

"I am your *prozia Maria* and that foolish old man sent me here to spy on you," she said. "And to cook and clean," she added as an afterthought.

"Prozia?" Brianna turned to Tom with a

quizzical look.

"Great aunt," he said.

He turned Brianna back into the room and a flush warmed his neck while he spoke to Maria. It would be obvious to anyone they'd been in bed together and Brianna's slumbrous eyes and flushed cheeks confirmed it. Even though they were technically married, guilt settled in his chest.

"We'll be out in a moment. Perhaps you could put some coffee on?"

"Nessuna fretta . . . no hurry. And I will cook for you *prima colazione*." A broad smile crossed her wrinkled face and she spread her arms wide. "You need to build up your energy again."

Wiping her eyes, she beamed at him with delight and turned back to the kitchen.

Tom nodded, bemused, and then followed Brianna to the bathroom attempting not to step on the bed sheet trailing along behind her. He closed the door quickly when she dropped the sheet. She stepped across to the shower and turned the jets on, at ease with her nudity. When she turned to him and held out her hand, he was tempted to forget all about the woman waiting in the kitchen.

"I have more family. She knew my mother. I am so, so happy." She looked across at him with a cheeky grin. "Want to wash my back?"

Tom gulped and resisted the invitation. He kept his gaze locked on her face trying to forget the feel of her bare body pressed against his minutes ago. "No, come on. We have to sort out what she's doing here."

"No one said the house came with a housekeeper and a cook," she said with a smile.

***

Ten minutes later, after they'd washed and dressed, the aroma of cooking enticed them to the kitchen. Maria clucked around, fussing until she was satisfied their plates were loaded with sausages stuffed with tomato and cheese. She filled a plate with delicate pastries from a basket in the kitchen and placed a large jug of what looked like crushed strawberry ice in the middle of the table.

Brianna leaned over the table and dipped her finger in and licked it.

"Mm. What is that?"

"*Granita* . . . from your strawberries." Aunt Maria pointed to the baskets hanging outside the kitchen window.

"My strawberries." Brianna turned to Tom with a delighted smile on her face.

After pouring fragrant coffee into three large mugs, Great Aunt Maria sat down at the table with them, and folded her hands across her ample stomach and beamed.

"He *ees* a stupid old man," she said in a firm voice. "And I will tell him so."

Tom looked across at Brianna, concern

spiking through his chest. He was keen to see her reaction. After all, here was yet another family member she hadn't known about. She'd been burdened with so much over the past few days, and they hadn't even had a chance to talk about them ending up in bed this morning. All agreements had flown out the window and now he had no idea where things stood between then.

Or where he wanted them to stand.

He needn't have worried. Brianna pointed to the food laid out on the table.

"Thank you. Can I call you Aunt Maria?" A wide smile crossed Brianna's face. "I can't quite get used to having a family. You will have to tell me all about everyone. I can't wait to meet them. Do they live on Lipari?"

Aunt Maria had a working knowledge of English and with Tom translating between them, they managed to get the gist of what she had said about the foolish old man—Brianna's grandfather

"He no trust." She wagged a finger. "He thinks you only want *ze* house."

The guilt stuck in Tom's throat and he looked up and caught Brianna's eye. She shook her head imperceptibly.

"But I was not going to not tell him what I saw." She cackled with delight. "Now I can tell him *ze* truth and tell him what I saw."

She drained her coffee and smacked her lips.

"Sunday—at the big house. You will come for dinner and meet all the family. *Si?*"

Tom looked across at Brianna and she nodded enthusiastically.

"*Si.*"

Aunt Maria gave Tom directions to find the big house in Lipari and what time to arrive. She gathered up her empty baskets after telling him she would be back each morning to prepare their evening meal. Tom and Brianna followed her to the door and waved to her as she wheeled her bicycle out the gate.

He turned to Brianna as Aunt Maria disappeared down the hill. The worry that had been niggling at him since he woke up came back in full force.

"Brianna. I think we need to have a chat about the terms of our agreement . . . now."

***

His less than subtle reminder of the need to discuss their agreement, and right now, fired her temper. For Christ's sake, they'd had sex, she'd just met her second relative and found out she had a whole family on the island waiting to meet her and he wanted to have a chat *now*. Deep down, she knew her anger was fuelled by her unexpected reaction to being with him this morning, but she buried the thought as deep as she could. Her life was complicated enough without going there.

Now.

Determined to present a light 'things aren't serious' front to him, she pushed her chair back and came around the table and placed her hands on his shoulders. Bending her head, she brushed her lips lightly across his.

"Now, Tomas, why do we need to talk?" She looked at him from under her lashes and ran her hand down his chest. "We already have a signed agreement. The only difference is that sex is now part of it. So if you want to add a—what do you call it?—condition, codicil, post script or whatever, just do it and I'll initial it. I've apologised to you for being a bitch and nothing else has changed. Has it?"

He looked at her without speaking and she felt like a right cow again, but she was damned if he was going to see the effect he'd had on her. She needed to put those feelings away and think about it later.

"So," she continued. "We're married. My grandfather is satisfied. You have your work at the marina. I have my book to write, and we also get the benefit of great sex."

She patted his shoulder, feigning a confidence she didn't have and turned away before he could see her pursed lips. She was as nervous as hell about what he wanted. If he wanted out of the agreement already, she didn't know what she'd do. And not just because of her mother's villa.

Gathering the dishes from the table, she walked across to the sink.

"Agreed?" she said evenly. She needed to be in control here.

When he didn't answer, she turned around and came face to face with him. He'd walked silently over to the sink in his bare feet. He placed his cup on the draining board, lined up neatly next to the other dishes. She waited for him to disagree, but he pushed his body against hers and bent his head. He wound her hair through his fingers and took her mouth in a hot kiss. Her head spun and she grasped at his shirt to keep her balance. Her back pressed into the cold stone of the sink and she moaned as his tongue plundered the depths of her mouth. Pulling back, he looked at her.

"We'll change the agreement. Friends with benefits."

Lost for words, Brianna stared at his back as he headed for the door. She reached up and placed her fingers against her lips. Control was back in Tom's hands.

And what hands they were.

Chapter Eleven

The hot morning sun burned Tom's skin as he rubbed the sandpaper up and down the bottom of the boat. Aunt Carmen had gone to Naples to visit her daughter, and he'd taken over the running of the marina. Matteo, the young boatman had shown him how to strip the paint and remove the old putty and caulking cotton in the boats lined up for re-caulking. He grinned to himself. If Nick and Alex could see him now they would give him a hard time. But the rhythmic motion of the sandpaper was what he needed to ease his temper this afternoon. It was much better than poring over the jumbled financial records. He'd borrowed Matteo's car and taken the boxes of financial records across to the villa. He had spread them out on an old table on the covered balcony, and it would give him something to focus on after dinner each night and stay away from Brianna.

He cursed himself for succumbing to her temptation so readily. The idea had been that he would come to Lipari and start living life on his terms, enjoy himself and he hadn't even been here a week and he had screwed up big time. But when he'd woken up with her in his arms this morning, a deep contentment had filled him.

For him it was always about more than just the sex, more than friends with benefits. And that's where he usually came unstuck. If that's all she was after, fine, she could damn well go without—he was not going to risk getting caught up in an emotional mess. He'd been there, and done that before. They'd added the friends with benefits clause to the agreement but she could run around the house naked for all he cared. He was not interested on those terms.

"Shit," he swore as he missed the timber and sliced his finger open on a bent nail.

Like hell he wasn't interested, but he was still going to ignore her. No way would he let her know the effect she was having on him. He wasn't going to risk being hurt again.

***

Later that evening, Brianna looked over her wine glass at Tom as they sat on the terrace overlooking the sea, appreciating the aroma of the spaghetti sauce Aunt Maria had left bubbling on the stove. She'd left instructions for adding the seafood from the refrigerator and cooking the spaghetti, which made her feel very clever, having been able to put the simple meal together.

A fat moon hung low over the ocean and silver trails shimmered on the long lazy swells that pushed into the shore. The salty tang of the sea breeze mixed with the aroma coming from the kitchen.

"I've never been able to cook, you know," she said to Tom, determined to engage him in conversation. He had answered each of her questions in monosyllables since he'd arrived home from Lipari late in the afternoon, and he'd not initiated one conversation. He'd disappeared straight into the bathroom and come out half an hour later in clean clothes. Trying to hide how his lack of conversation was bothering her, she prattled on.

"Aunt Maria left very simple instructions so I hope it turns out."

"I'm sure it will." He raised the glass to his lips and stared out over the sea.

She couldn't hold back any longer. "Oh for pity's sake, stop acting like a spoiled wee child who can't get his own way."

He raised his eyebrows. For a moment she thought he wasn't going to answer. When he swallowed and his Adam's apple bobbed, she realised he was trying not to react to her goading.

"I think you have a bit of growing up to do, speaking of 'wee' children," he said, picking up the carafe and gesturing to her glass. Brianna burned up, not liking the look on his face nor the tone of his voice. She ignored his offer.

Why?" she asked. "Because I'm honest about my feelings and I know what I want and I go for it?"

His mouth, the same mouth that had taken her to paradise and back that very morning, turned up in a patient smile.

"No, because you can't accept that when I'm being honest about my feelings, I'm entitled to my opinion. I think if we sleep together it's going to stuff up our arrangement. That's the way I feel and you'll have to accept it because you won't change my mind."

The warmth of a flush burned its way up her neck and she blessed her olive complexion. How dare he try to make her feel bad about seducing him this morning?

"I don't recall you thinking that way earlier," she said coldly. "In fact, I recall you were a more than willing participant." She locked her gaze with his and was pleased to see a pulse flicked in his cheek and twin spots of colour darkened his skin. "And you added the friends with benefits bit to the agreement."

"So we've got all bases covered then," he said. "If you're happy for me to keep living here, I'll be most grateful. I'll sort out the finances, you can write your book, and when the right time comes, I'll head back to Australia or wherever the mood takes me. You'll have your villa and we'll both be happy."

"Fine." She tossed her head. "That suits me fine too." She was still a bit unnerved, never having felt so connected with anyone before. He'd ignored her mention of the 'benefits' but she'd be damned if she's bring up the sex again.

They both sat there glaring at each other until a bubble of mirth escaped from Brianna's mouth.

"I'm sorry." She put her hand up to her quivering lips. "I've never been able to stay mad. I *always* lose an argument. My brother and sister always won and I had to do their chores because they would bet me I couldn't keep a straight face."

Finally, Tom smiled back at her. "It's not such a bad thing. I was always the serious one in our family. Must be a personality type I inherited."

He stood and came and kneeled beside her chair, and picked up her hand. A frisson of warmth ran up her arm. "You bring out the worst in me, Brianna. Do you think you can put up with me *and* my hang-ups for a few months?"

"Oh, Tom, you don't have any hang-ups. And there's nothing to put up with. There's not a lot you don't know about me." Brianna looked down at his hand and ran her thumb over a cut on his finger. "Look, I'll be honest. I don't do emotion well. I do sex, I am a loyal friend, but I don't do emotion." She laughed when she saw the expression of his face. "It's okay, I have a very happy life, and I live it on my terms. Now, let's make a new deal."

"Agreement version three? Let me go and get the piece of paper."

Brianna laughed and shook her head. "Forget the paper. Stay living here with me. I need to convince that cantankerous old grandfather of mine that I really am his granddaughter and this house is mine. I want it and I'm going to keep it. I want to find out as much as I can about my mother and why she gave me up. There's all that stuff of hers I haven't even looked at yet." She squeezed his hand. "And I'll help you chill out and we'll work on your list and have a great time together, and then you can pay me back." She burst out laughing at the sceptical look on his face. "You are so easy to read. Don't worry, there's no sex in my equation."

"I'll need to pay you back for giving me a roof over my head."

"Help me get organised so I can finish my book and make the deadline."

"But I'm no writer. I have no idea how to go about writing a book."

"I can do the writing . . . it's the time management, and as much as I hate to admit it to you, some list making would speed up my output. I tend to stuff around and miss most of my deadlines.

This is my last chance before I'm in breach of my contract." She dropped her head. "And I've already spent the advance."

He nodded. "Is it a psychology text book?"

"You could say that." She avoided a direct answer. He wasn't quite ready for the subject matter of her book. She didn't want him running away yet; she needed him to stay around until her grandfather accepted her and she was sure she could keep the villa. Plus, she was getting quite used to having him around.

"And Tom, one more wee favour?" She reached up and ran her fingers down the side of his face. "You know, I really, really want this house. You don't know how much it means to me to have the opportunity to find out about my real mother. So when we see my grandfather, would you keep up the 'loving husband, so much in love with me, you can't keep your hands off me' act?"

He let go of her hand and stood and moved away to the edge of the balcony.

"As long as you keep your side of the bargain. No more early morning visits to make it real."

"I promise. No more friends with benefits." She tipped her head to the side. "I'll wait until *you* ask."

He rolled his eyes at her.

"You, madam, are incorrigible and I can

smell burning sauce."

With a squeal she ran into the kitchen and whipped the saucepan off the stove before it boiled over.

***

Tom sat back and wiped his mouth with the linen napkin. Brianna had set up a small dining table out on the balcony and they made plans for her writing routine while they ate the *spaghetti marinara.*

"Now we've got your writing space organised, do you think you might need to get Internet access here?"

She shook her head. "No, too much temptation to chat instead of writing. I'll come to Lipari with you to the Internet café when I need to contact my publisher."

He was surprised at her self-discipline. She tipped her head forward and flicked her thick braid over her shoulder. It was less tempting for him with her hair tied back, but he still remembered how the tendrils had brushed against his bare skin. As it was, he was having a hard enough time forgetting how her skin felt, the taste of her, and how she'd pulsed around him. He swallowed and desperately tried to think of something other than reaching for her and kissing her exposed neck. He grasped at the first thing that came into his mind.

"Oh, by the way, your aunt sent a message

to the marina and said someone will pick us up here on Sunday for the dinner at your grandfather's place."

Brianna sat with her chin propped in her hands gazing out over the water, her eyes reflecting the moonlight and she spoke softly. "I'm a bit nervous about meeting him again, you know. He is such a sad man." Her body was outlined in the soft moonlight and the gentle swell of her breast under the loose T-shirt drew his gaze.

Tom stood suddenly and dropped his napkin to the table fighting the surge of desire pulsing through him.

"I'm going to bed." His chair scraped on the tiled balcony. If he didn't leave now, he was going to do something he'd regret and break every damn promise he'd made to himself. "Good night."

"Good night, Tom."

He lay on his back for a long time, watching the moonlight play across the ceiling, angry at himself and frustrated, wondering what sort of a fool he was. He'd never been so fascinated by a woman. She'd breathed life into every minute of the day. She was willing and had made her position as clear as day so why was he hesitating?

He didn't need that emotional stuff. It sounded too much like commitment to him and he wasn't going anywhere near that.

***

"You can have the bathroom first," Brianna called out from the room she'd set up with a table and her laptop. Tom stripped off his sweat-soaked work shirt and threw it into the old stone tub in the laundry room off the back balcony. In less than a week they had settled into' a routine and there'd been no major fireworks between them. And he'd managed to keep his hands off her.

Aunt Carmen was still in Naples and he'd spent the past four days working on the boats. Instead of catching the old bus back to Cannetto today, he'd left early and walked along the cliff path between the villages. The view was spectacular and he'd promised himself a trip to climb the volcano, which puffed out white smoke all day. Another one off the list.

"Thanks," he called back. "I'll be quick. Maria said we'll get picked up about five."

He stripped off, surprised by the deep tan he'd acquired in a few days. He shaved for the first time in a week. Brianna had been quieter than usual the past couple of nights and he suspected she was nervous about meeting her grandfather again. Either that or it was sexual frustration. He knew all about that. He couldn't get her out of his mind, and knowing she was just through the wall in the next room each night was killing him.

He turned the water off in the shower and jumped as the door opened before he could reach for a towel. And then he realised there were no towels hanging on the rail.

"Sorry, I took the towels out this morning and washed them." Brianna stepped into the bathroom and handed him a clean towel, and broke into a huge grin when he grabbed it and wrapped it around his hips.

"Wow, great tan." She turned and headed for the door." Don't be embarrassed. I've seen it all before." Gently closing the door, she laughed. "I've got a brother, remember."

Tom shook his head. She was so confident and so full of the joy of life, he had no doubt she would have her grandfather and the rest of her family under her spell before the night was out.

Christ knows, she's got me sucked right in.

The most explosive sex of his life had left him wanting more. Once he finally got to sleep each night, he dreamed about her and those magic hands. It took all his will power to stop himself from knocking on her door, climbing into bed with her, and taking up where his imagination had left off.

Earlier in the week she'd shared some of her work with him and he'd seen another side of her. He'd wandered over to her desk to help her with a printer jam and read the chapter list on a piece of paper stuck in the printer.

This giggly, free-spirited girl was writing a textbook on sex therapy. He shook his head and smiled. A couple of weeks ago he would have run a mile but their conversations had shown him a different side to her and he'd developed a respect for her knowledge and her obvious clinical experience. Her exuberance for her subject had impressed him and she'd challenged him with some questionnaires and shown him the fun side of being psycho-analysed by her. It had got him thinking and he'd mulled over the couple of failed relationships in his past as he'd worked out in the fresh air this week. Like everything he did, he'd focused on them too much before they had developed. His total approach was wrong.

No more.

Half an hour later, Tom and Brianna waited together on the balcony for the promised lift. A small crescent moon hung low over the horizon. The pungent aroma of herbs surrounded them, crushed underfoot as they crossed the stone path.

"Do you know who's picking us up? Do you think it will be him?" She ran her fingers through her loose curls, a sure sign she was nervous. "My grandfather . . . *Nonno*, I mean."

"I don't know. Maria said to be ready at five."

She smoothed her dress down with nervous hands. A deep plunging back left her tanned skin bare. Tom put his arm around her and tried to ignore the jolt that went straight to his groin when he touched her warm, satiny skin. Her loose curls tumbled over her bare shoulders and she smelled of coconut. "It'll be fine. I'll be the loving husband and I'll watch out for you. If he gets nasty, we'll come home early, even if we have to walk."

She snuggled into him. "You are a good man, Tom Richards."

The purring of a car motor coming slowly up the hill caught Tom's attention and he whistled in appreciation. He gently turned her around and pointed to the car silhouetted by the setting sun.

"Not bad," he said. "Not bad at all."

"What is it?" she asked.

"A C-class Mercedes Benz coupe. Very nice." He had considered one of them before purchasing his latest BMW back home.

She shrugged. "A car's a car."

"Oh, you Philistine. It's a thing of beauty." He laughed. "I can see I need to educate you. Just because I've been depending on that old rattle trap of a bus to get around, I still appreciate a fine motor, and you and I are about to have a ride in one of the best."

The large white car drew to a halt beside them, and Tom glanced across at Brianna. She choked back a laugh when a middle-aged man wearing a chauffeur's uniform and a cap with a gold insignia stepped out of the car and bowed to them.

"Signore, Signorina." He opened the back

door and gestured for them to enter. Brianna slid in and Tom joined her and placed his arm around her.

"You never know, the hired help may have been sent to spy on you, too," he whispered with a smile. Besides it was an innocent opportunity to touch her.

"Why would my *nonno* send a hired car to pick us up?" she whispered back.

"I'm not so sure it's a hired car. I think we may be in for some surprises tonight, so best prepare yourself." He squeezed her shoulder appreciating the way she tucked in under his arm. A warm contentment filled him. The driver turned the car around in the drive and headed down the hill toward Lipari. They cruised through the town and climbed the hill to the west, where a large villa on top of the ridge was bathed in light.

"Holy Moses, don't tell me that's my grandfather's house."

"I think it's more than a house."

Brianna reached over and gripped his hand. "I don't know if I can do this."

"You'll be fine. Remember how sweet Aunt Maria is . . . and I'll be with you to look out for you."

The car turned through a large set of ornate gates that opened automatically when they approached and then down a sweeping driveway flanked by a low hedge. Bright spotlights highlighted ornate statues of gods and goddesses placed at regular intervals.

The car drew to a halt in front of a small fountain, and the chauffeur opened the door on the passenger side. Brianna slid across the black leather seat, hitching her dress down over her long, bare legs. Tom followed, pleased she'd discarded her usual garb of khaki cargo pants and T-shirts. Apart from their wedding it was only the second time he'd seen her in a dress. With legs like that, legs that went forever, she should wear dresses every day.

"Quit gawking and be a good husband." She grabbed his arm and pulled him closer just as Aunt Maria came running down the steps to greet them.

"*Benvenuto*." She clutched at Tom's arm and pulled him down and kissed both his cheeks.

"And my *cara nipote.* "Aunt Maria looped her arm through Brianna's. "Now you come and meet your *famiglia*."

Tom hurried to catch up to them and took Brianna's other arm. He straightened his back, stiffening his resolve to protect his 'wife' from any unpleasantness that may ensue. Maria led them through a marble foyer with a massive chandelier hanging from a domed ceiling.

"Close your mouth, Bri." He leaned over and jabbed her in the ribs.

They followed Maria and passed through whitewashed arches and over cool ceramic floors until they reached the back of the house. The view looked out over the mountainous interior of the volcanic island. A solarium, a tennis court, and a lawn for playing bocce were surrounded by a large garden of citrus and olive trees.

"It's like something from the movies," she whispered. "Is this really *his* place?" She frowned as she looked across the garden.

"We'll soon find out."

"I can't understand this. What's the big deal with him wanting my little house?"

Aunt Maria stepped out into a shady arbour where dozens of people of all ages stood around chatting. Tom held Brianna back and pulled her close. He closed his eyes and listened. It reminded him of home, and for a brief moment he missed his boisterous family.

"What's wrong?"

"Nothing," he said lowering his head and kissing her briefly on the lips. "Just playing the loving husband."

Brianna reached up and touched his face and looked adoringly into his eyes as Aunt Maria led them across to her *nonno*.

"*Signore* Caranto." Tom stepped forward and held out his hand, and was pleased to see the old man smile. His hand was pumped enthusiastically and Tom pulled Brianna forward with his free hand.

"Brianna, say hello to your grandfather."

He held his breath as the old man and his granddaughter stood and took stock of each other. Eventually the old man nodded and held his arm out to her.

"Nonno." She nodded and linked her arm through his and held her other hand out to Tom. He gripped it tightly and followed them out to the waiting crowd.

Two hours later, Tom stepped into a dim corner of the lawn and sipped his drink. Brianna had kissed him, touched his arm, ran her fingers up his back, ruffled his hair and gripped his thigh on numerous occasions throughout the meal, and the old man had not taken his sharp gaze from them for one minute.

His body was humming and the blood was pumping through at a rate of knots. He needed some space and some fresh air. His attention was caught by Brianna's familiar laugh drifting across the garden.

Jeez, even the sound of her voice gave him a hard on.

He closed his eyes and gathered his thoughts, trying to dispel the desire shooting through his body. Playing the loving husband was not such a good idea. It had played havoc with his self-control all night. He'd squirmed like an adolescent right through dinner as he'd been introduced to cousin after cousin.

A whiff of coconut alerted him to her presence. He opened his eyes and his gaze was captured and held. Brianna pressed against him and looped her arms around his neck, her bare thigh brushing against his leg.

He groaned and she reached up and pressed her lips against his. "One last convincing display and we've done it," she murmured against his mouth. "Look at him, standing up on the balcony. The old man hasn't taken his eyes off us all night."

"I guess I can act like a besotted husband for a few more minutes." Her lips parted and he kissed her soundly, his tongue delving into her mouth. When he could take no more, he pulled away and gently turned her back to the lawn where her newly met cousins were taking their leave.

Tom and Brianna made their farewells and fielded many invitations to dinner at different villages around the island. There was no doubt the long lost granddaughter was a success and had been welcomed by the rest of the family with open arms. It was a damn shame the old fellow was still so reserved.

The driver was waiting for them in the car, and Tom held the door for Brianna as she stepped into the back seat. For a moment, he thought of traveling in the front to put a bit of distance between them. He slid in next to her and sat next to the window as far from her as he could. Brianna didn't appear to notice his lack of conversation, and chattered all the way home. He was grateful to have his attention taken away from the raging hard on that had been with him for most of the night.

"And I found out what the problem is between your Aunt Carmen and *Nonno*." The affectionate term for her grandfather came naturally now and he smiled when she lowered her voice to a whisper. "Apparently, they had a thing before your uncle came along and swept her off her feet . . . and they haven't spoken since."

"That explains why he didn't come to lunch after we got married," Tom said. He jumped when Brianna reached across and put her hand on his thigh.

"And not only that. I am so excited."

You and me both, thought Tom. He removed her hand from his thigh and put it back in her lap, but she didn't seem to notice.

"Bella—she's Aunt Maria's youngest—told me a little bit about my mother. She was close to her before she left the island. Apparently, when she came back, the villa was a holiday base for her."

"Maybe she left because she was pregnant with you?"

"Maybe." Her voice was wistful. "There's still an awful lot I don't know." She touched his leg

179

again. "Now how about you? Did you have fun tonight?"

"I suppose that's one way of putting it," he said and tipped his head back and closed his eyes. She pulled her hand back as though it was burned.

The rest of the short journey home was completed without another word exchanged. They waved the driver off and crossed the courtyard to the gate. Brianna took the key from her bag, handed it to Tom, and stood beside him while he turned it in the lock. The gate creaked open. The sexual tension in the air was so thick he found it difficult to catch his breath. He bent and removed his loafers and placed them neatly by the door. She strolled ahead of him and reached for the light switch. He caught her hand.

"Leave the lights off."

Brianna turned and looked at him, her eyes wide. She didn't speak and made no move toward him. Pulling her hard against him, he ran his hands down her bare back. When she reached up and grabbed his hair and leaned into him, her lips were a breath away from his. He lowered his head, and her lips opened beneath his, her hands moving beneath his shirt. Tom groaned as her nails raked down his back. Desire overwhelmed him and he deepened the kiss, wanting, needing his mouth on hers.

"You are the most beautiful woman I have ever known," he murmured against her mouth.

"You've bewitched me. You're in my blood."

His voice was low and husky, and it was as though someone else was speaking. A spark of mutual need passed between them and her heart pounded against his chest. She leaned against him for a moment and then lifted her head and smiled up at him as he lowered his mouth to hers again.

**

Brianna accepted Tom's kiss and wondered if he could feel the thumping of her heart. He kissed her slowly, and she tried to catch her breath as his lips moved gently against hers. Before she could take a breath, he lifted her in his arms and she wrapped her legs around him. She laughed as he walked into her bedroom.

He put her on the bed and looked down at her.

"Wait," she murmured.

He stiffened and she laughed and pointed to the bedside table. "In the top drawer."

Within seconds, the foil packet discarded on the floor with his clothes and Brianna chuckled. "Mr. Neat and Tidy forgot to fold his clothes."

"I don't think he'll need them for a while," he said and reached for her again.

Chapter Twelve

Brianna pushed her hair back from her face and wiped the perspiration from her brow with the back of her arm. She stood, stretched, and cracked her knuckles. God, her back was sore. She'd been sitting at the desk for five hours, but she had finished the three chapters her publisher had requested. The first draft of the whole book was almost complete and she hoped to get it away by the end of the week. She'd followed the schedule Tom had written out for her to the minute, determined to show him she could be organised and wasn't a complete airhead.

Why she wanted to impress him with her efficiency, she couldn't explain. She didn't want to be super organised like him, although she had to admit the Tom who was spending each day at the marina was way more relaxed than the man she'd met on the plane.

Smiling to herself, she thought of the routine they had fallen into over the past couple of months. Aunt Carmen had gone off to Naples again visiting friends now she had sold the business. Tom had taken over the day-to-day running of the boats, but the financial records were still piled on the table on the balcony.

He'd moved into her bedroom after the night at *Nonno*'s villa. Their days were spent working and their nights were full of passion. She smiled and plugged in her external hard drive—another lesson she'd learned from him. The external drive whirred as she stared through the window with her chin propped in her hand. A cloud of dust down the hill caught her attention. She stood and peered out the window to see who was coming. What the hell was it?

She stepped out onto the balcony and an old rusty bicycle appeared over the crest of the hill. White teeth in a tanned face surrounded by unruly black hair flashed at her in a wide grin at her as the old bicycle creaked closer. The front wheel wobbled from side to side as Tom rode up the hill toward the villa. Brianna put her hand over her mouth, waiting for the inevitable fall. She giggled at the intense concentration on his face as he fought to control the wobble.

Another thing to tick off his crazy list.

He pushed the last twenty yards with a loud whoop. She ran to the front gate and opened it so he could ride through without stopping. She ran to him and hugged him after he'd propped the bike against the wall.

"You did it! Where on earth did you find the old bike?"

"Ah . . . your grandfather gave it to me." He avoided looking at her.

She pulled back and her heart plummeted. "What were you doing there? How come I wasn't invited?" No matter how hard she tried, her relationship with her *Nonno* was going nowhere. He was still very reserved with her and their meetings were always tense.

"Maria wanted me to see him about some of her business and it was in an old shed at the back of his villa."

"And he gave it to you?"

"Well, I offered to buy it."

But no matter how cross she was with Tom for visiting her grandfather without her, she still laughed.

"You paid for it? It's almost a relic. It should be in that museum near Aunt Carmen's. He's so filthy rich, I can't believe he made you pay for it. "

He stood straight and smiled a devastating smile.

"Bri, come here." He reached out and pulled her into a close hug. "He's not a bad old stick. You have to make more of an effort with him."

"I've done as much as I can, Tom. It's him, he just won't accept *me*." She looked up at him and all mirth had fled. Being unable to connect with her grandfather upset her a lot, more than she was going to let on. She'd tried to speak to him about her mother and he'd used the language barrier, and the only information Aunt Maria would share was how they had been close, but not close enough to know her secrets. The few possessions of her mother's in the house had not given any clue to Rosa's life.

"When he's not got his eagle eye on us, he just ignores me. I might as well go back to Scotland when I finish the book."

"I thought you were keen to stay here." He raised a quizzical brow. She swallowed and warmth suffused her face. She avoided his gaze and turned away, walking back to the kitchen.

"I am but I have to earn a living." There was no way Tom was going to know she'd thought about staying on the island after the book was done so she could stay here with him. She quickly changed the subject. "Now what's for dinner? I was working when Aunt Maria left, so dinner's a surprise."

Brianna looked up at him as he followed her into the kitchen. He had a silly grin plastered on his face and folded his arms across his chest. "I crossed another thing off the list today and you haven't even noticed." He dropped his knapsack and bent to pull out a piece of paper. Her gaze wandered to his tight butt. A few weeks of manual work and he was in good shape.

"Well, two more things." He waved the

paper in her face. "And if you count tomorrow . . . three things."

"What else have you done?" God, she thought, talk about a role reversal. She was turning into a mother hen.

"Close your eyes," he said.

"Why?"

"Trust me, Bri." His deep voice sent a thrill through her. "Close your eyes."

She did as he asked and stood quietly until the warmth of his breath fanned her face.

"Now you can open them." All she could see was a riot of black curls in front of her. His hair had grown and was becoming more unruly every day.

"I took my specs off. I can't see a thing. Tell me?"

With a flourish, he pushed his hair back and she gasped.

"Freakin' hell. I don't believe it."

A small gold ring worthy of a pirate hung from his left ear lobe.

"Jesus, Mary and Joseph. Tom, you did it." She bent over and doubled up laughing uncontrollably. He stood there with a grin on his face.

"Yes, I did it and it hurt."

"Well, why did you do it, you silly man?"

"Because it was on my list. And I can

always take it out when I go back home."

Her mood plummeted and she realised they would go their separate ways eventually. She couldn't stay here forever. They'd divorce and he would be out of her life.

"Come here. He wrapped his arms around her, and rested his chin on the top of her head. "Why the sad face? Does the earring look that bad?" He tried to get her to smile.

"I know it's almost over . . . and we've had such fun. I'm going to miss you." She spread her arms wide and spun around out of his arms. "And all this."

"It doesn't have to end, Bri. We could always stay here."

She laughed. "Don't tease me. I said I was going home when I finished the book and I am."

He gripped her upper arms and his hands were warm as he pulled her hard against her chest. "Now tell me you aren't going to miss this?"

Warm lips slid across her check and he blew in her ear. Goose bumps skittered down her arms and she shivered.

"I need a shower," he murmured close to her ear. "Come and wash my back?"

She stepped back and looked deep into those blue eyes, unable to resist him.

God, she had no will power when he was around her.

"I have to finish backing up my work," she said, her breathing ragged.

"What are you up to? Tantric sex or erogenous zones?" He kissed her neck as his hands wandered lower.

Aroused, but preoccupied with her thoughts, she pushed his hands away. Turning her back to him, she walked across to the large window and gazed out over the sea. "Go have a shower. I'll back up my work and check what Italian delight is in the refrigerator for dinner." She watched as he peeled his T-shirt off. A shaft of heat lodged between her thighs. "And then I'll come and wash your back."

She headed for the computer and then remembered what he'd said. "What was next on the list?"

"We're both taking the day off tomorrow and climbing a volcano."

She shook her head in disbelief. She'd created a monster . . . or at the very least a dare devil.

"I suppose I can spare a day to explore with you, and Tom, I so appreciate what you've done to help me. You'll have that list completely checked off before you know it."

***

Tom turned the shower on full blast and stepped in. For a moment, he was tempted to turn it to cold—to quell his desire and then decided he wasn't going to. He would wait for Brianna to join him and then afterward he was going to talk to her, uninterrupted by the desire that exploded when they were in the same room. Sharing her bed since the night of the dinner at her grandfather's villa had been amazing, and although they had spent many pleasurable nights and mornings, they'd avoided any discussion of the future.

A future he could not envision without her now.

It was time for a serious talk. The past couple of months had been the happiest he'd ever been, and he'd be damned if he was going to let her go. She'd let her guard down before. Now it was time to convince her they had a future together.

He stood under the sharp needles of spray and tipped his head back letting the warm water run down his body. The door of the bathroom opened. She was going to join him after all. The earring must have made him irresistible.

Brianna appeared in the bathroom, her face drained of colour and he knew immediately something was very wrong. His gaze dropped to his phone clutched in her hand.

"Tom . . . it's . . . it's your mother on the phone. She wants to talk to you. There's been an accident."

His stomach clenched as he stepped out of the shower, grabbing a towel as he reached for the phone.

"A car accident." Her voice broke and tears rolled down her cheeks. "Your brother's fiancée."

Chapter Thirteen

The ferry receded into the distance and Brianna touched a hand to her lips. Despite his grief, Tom had held her close and kissed her for a long time before boarding the ferry. Her skin still tingled where he'd gripped her. He'd pushed her away gently and stared down at her, rubbing his hands up and down her sides, as though he was reluctant to let go.

"Promise me you'll be here when I come back?" he asked.

"I've still got three chapters to do before I go home."

"I'll be back in a week or so. No longer."

She stood on tiptoes and kissed him again, and pushed him toward the boarding ramp as the ferry horn warned that departure was imminent.

"Are you sure you are going to be all right by yourself?" His brow creased in a worried frown.

"I've lived alone for ten years. I'll be fine. You worry about taking care of yourself and your family. Ring me when you arrive."

"Don't forget to charge your phone," he

said with the first glimmer of a smile since the phone call from his mother. He held her gaze until the ferry accelerated with a churning of water and disappeared around the headland.

After saying goodbye she made her way to the Internet café, where she emailed her completed chapters to the publisher and answered the many emails waiting for her. She smiled at the messages from her family.

Brianna. We know you are a bad letter writer, but at least email and tell us you're still in Italy?

She replied to her mother and sent messages to Phil and her sister, and to as many friends she could find in her address book.

Finally she admitted to herself she was avoiding going home to the empty villa. It wouldn't be the same by herself. Placing her back-up drive in her knapsack and checking she had water in her drink bottle, she decided to walk home along the cliff path between the villages.

Thoughts crowded her mind as she wandered along the path, the warm sun beating down on her head. A mass of wildflowers covered the cliff down to the rocky beach below, and she paused to pick one every so often until she had a small posy in her hands. At the halfway point, she rounded a headland and Mt. Stromboli appeared before her, rising majestically out of the ocean, plumes of smoke puffing from the live volcano.

Tears filled her eyes. She sat on the grass and she wiped them away angrily. They should have been over there today, climbing the volcano together and crossing another thing off Tom's stupid list.

Life sucked, it really did.

Her heart went out to Tom's brother. Losing his fiancée so young would be so hard to bear. Even though she didn't know him, she knew from the way Tom spoke, he thought the world of him and no one deserved the grief he was going through. She was missing Tom so much already. She had to get her act together. It would be good practice for when she went back home. Okay, so she'd miss him for a while and then she'd get on with her life.

She didn't need this emotional crap.

She'd got on quite well by herself over the last ten years. She had a great job, she had friends and her adopted family was always there for her…and now she had a second family as well. Always a free spirit and that's the way she wanted to stay. Families were too complicated. She wasn't going to get tied up with anyone for life.

She wiped away the tears that wouldn't stop falling and then picked up her knapsack and marched toward Cannetto. There was a book to be finished and she would edit it as quickly as she could. When Tom came back, they would do their Stromboli trip and then she would go back to Scotland and get on with her life . . . alone.

Italy had been a nice interlude, even if she hadn't found out much about her mother. At least she knew where she came from, and she had a nice villa for her vacation every year.

She walked up the hill to the villa and groaned when she reached the crest.

Oh shit, not today.

The white Mercedes was parked outside the gate and her grandfather stood stiffly beside it. Brianna slowly covered the distance between them and stood next to him. He gestured to the driver and the uniformed man went around to the back, opened the trunk, and lifted out a large cardboard box.

The old man nodded at her. "Brianna." His voice made her name sound so musical.

"Nonno." She nodded back and stood waiting to see what he wanted.

"I come in?"

"I suppose. If you want." She shrugged and turned to the ornate metal gate. If he wasn't prepared to make an effort, she was just about ready to give up. She pulled the key from her knapsack, and was surprised when he held out his hand and took the key, opening the gate for her. The driver followed them in, and her grandfather gestured for him to put the box on the table and wait outside.

Brianna waited for him to speak first. She was in no mood for any more emotional stuff. He could say what he wanted and leave, although her gaze kept flicking to the box the driver had placed on the table.

He surprised her again by walking over to the sink and filling the coffeepot and putting it on the stove. He knew his way around; it was obvious he'd been here before. She sat and waited, and didn't speak, but surprisingly the silence was not uncomfortable.

The tantalising aroma of coffee wafted past her nose as he brought the coffee pot to the table and then went to the cupboard and removed the biscuit tin Maria kept filled for them. He carefully poured the coffee, and pushed the cream and sugar and a plate of biscuits in front of her.

She looked up and her stomach clenched when she saw his lips quivering. She dropped her head as tears filled her eyes and threatened to spill.

"Mia caro . . ." His voice quavered.

She was *not* going to make this easy for him and she lifted her head, holding his gaze refusing to let the tears fall. Finally, her shoulders sagged and she pointed to the box.

"What is it?"

He smiled and spoke in broken English.

"Your mama, she must have loved you very much. But your father go. It was a . . . how you say…shame?"

"Disgrace?" She filled in the missing word.

"*Si* . . . disgrace. She no tell us . . . her mama and I. She went away for years and when she come back, we still not know about you."

"Not until she die . . ." He wiped his eyes with a shaking finger, and Brianna wished Tom was here with her.

"And I get box from bank in Naples. She send there when she get sick."

Brianna stopped fighting the tears. Her throat ached too much and they rolled down her cheeks. It was only a few months now since her mother had died. She'd had thirty years to find her and she'd failed. Smashing her hand down on the table, the cups rattled in their saucers.

"Why didn't you tell me this sooner?" She put her head down on the table and buried her face in her arms as the tears came. "You've known the whole time I was your granddaughter? I thought you doubted me." Wrenching sobs overtook her and she struggled for breath. A soft gnarled hand rubbed her arm as her grandfather reached over and touched her. For the first time in her life someone of her own flesh and blood comforted her and warmth filled her chest.

"She was good daughter . . . and she would have love you very much."

"Yeah, sure," said Brianna. "I would rather

have known her than had this." She sat up and gestured to the house around them.

"You see." He patted the box. "I wait outside. You come see me."

###

He stood and walked from the house, and moments later the metal gate clanged shut behind him. Then there was only the whisper of the sea caressing the sand below the hill.

Brianna didn't move. She stared at the box for five minutes as though there were a cobra inside ready to strike the minute she opened it. Her fingers tingled in anticipation, but trepidation took over. She went over to the sink, filled a glass with water, and sat at the table. She reached out and ran her fingers along the edge of the box.

Lifting the lid, she put it aside and waited a moment.

Oh God, I wish Tom was here. It would be so much easier. And then she got cross with herself for wanting him.

A lavender scent drifted across her nostrils and tempted her. She stood and peeked into the large cardboard box. Inside was a smaller box tied with mauve ribbon. She reached in and lifted it out, surprised at its weight.

Her name was written across the top of the lid, and for a moment she thought it was her own handwriting. Shaking her head in confusion, she looked closely and realised that although the writing was very similar to hers, some of the letters were formed with ornate loops, which she didn't use.

She undid the ribbon and removed the lid. A soft gasp escaped her lips. More than two dozen small packages were neatly labelled with each year from her birth up until one year ago.

She picked up one package at random and three photographs fell out. The top one was a photograph of her graduation, standing with her adoptive parents outside Edinburgh University.

She remembered the day well. Jennifer and Jim had seemed so proud that day and had insisted on a photograph, asking a passer-by to snap them before they went to a hotel in the Lawnmarket for a celebratory lunch. She turned the photo over and recognised Jennifer's handwriting.

Brianna, Jim and Jennifer. Graduation, 2002.

Photograph after photograph chronicled her life. All the milestones, each birthday and Christmas, and many random shots of her playing the fool. She smiled as the memories came flooding back. Each photograph captured the essence of her and the happiness of her family life.

Bloody hell.

She didn't know whether to be ecstatic or devastated that her mother *had* known her. Why in the hell hadn't she contacted her, especially when

Brianna had tried so hard to find her?

Angrily picking up the photographs, she went to throw them back in the box and give them back to her *nonno*. She knew enough now. Her mother had known all about her, she'd left her a villa, but didn't care enough about her to even contact her. At the bottom of the box, was an envelope with *Brianna* written across the front in the same stylish handwriting. The lavender paper was delicate, and the folds were creased as though it had been read and refolded many times. She reached for it and unfolded it with shaking fingers, and started to read before she could think.

Chapter Fourteen

Tom bowed his head and kept his arm firmly around Alex's back as the pallbearers brought Emily's coffin down the wide aisle of the church. The last time he'd stood at his brother's side it had been a joyous occasion at Nick's wedding.

Now, he looked across and caught Nick's eye, and a silent message of support passed between them. They linked hands behind Alex as their younger brother's shoulders shook and the grief of his fiancée's death overwhelmed him. The music swelled as Emily's father and brothers brought the coffin down the middle aisle of the church toward the vestibule and the waiting hearse.

Tom swallowed his grief and focused his thoughts on Brianna. If this had happened to him, he was sure he wouldn't survive it. The depths of his feelings for her hit him like a punch in his chest. He loved her, and by God, he was not going to let her go. He had to get back to Lipari Island and convince her that they had something special. It shouldn't be treated flippantly and discarded.

The situation and the grief had firmed his resolve. Brianna was his wife and they were right for each other. Her joy of life brought out the best in him, and he knew he was good for her. They laughed constantly and all their time together, even from those first few hours on the plane had been special. For the first time in his life, he loved a woman . . . unconditionally. He was confident he could convince her to marry him, for real this time.

"Come on, mate." He leaned over to his younger brother. "Time to go outside."

The three brothers followed Emily's mother and sister to the door and stood quietly in the little churchyard as the coffin slid into the back of a hearse.

***

Tom stood alone at the window of his parent's large living room and the noise of muted conversations washed over him. Tessa had offered the use of their home for the wake and he knew Emily's family appreciated the gesture.

"Tom?"

Warm fingers squeezed his arm and he turned to see Lissy standing next to him.

"We're all so pleased you were able to get home in time for the funeral," she said. "You'll be tired after the flight and today, well, today has been so very hard for everybody."

"Of course I came. We all had to be here for Alex."

Although she smiled, her eyes filled with tears. "It really brings the uncertainty of life home with a vengeance when someone is taken so young."

Tom hugged Lissy and held her close for a moment. "Where's Nick?"

"He's out with Alex saying goodbye to Emily's parents." She stepped back and patted her swelling abdomen. "He wanted me to stay inside. He wraps me in cotton wool."

"I haven't offered my congratulations. I'm very happy for both of you."

"We weren't going to share the news till we were all together at Christmas, but well . . . everyone can see it for themselves now." She looked up at Tom, her eyes wide and shook her head. "And you . . . look at you. You look amazing, so healthy and relaxed."

He laughed grimly. "Come on, Lissy, be honest. I'm not such a stuffed shirt anymore."

"No, I didn't mean that. It's just the hair and the tan and the earring. Well . . . we—" she stumbled over her words "Let's say we nearly didn't recognise you at the airport. You look so different. Out of the three brothers, I never thought you'd turn into the bad boy." She reached up and her hand was warm against his neck as she flicked his earring. "But the main thing is, despite our grief today, you look happy. Tell me about Brianna."

Tom thought about the best way to describe her.

"Brianna is full of life. She sees the good in every situation and she makes me laugh. It's been a tough few months for her in some ways—she's tried to find out about her mother, but there seems to be a real secret there—but she's a real Pollyanna." He touched the black curls tumbling past his collar. "She makes me laugh at myself and I've done things I would never have thought of doing before. I've loved every moment of it."

Lissy laughed. "Too much information."

"Oh, God no." He hurried to correct himself. "I've done physical things . . . fun things."

"You're getting me more intrigued by the minute." She smiled at him and turned to Tessa who had walked over to join them.

"Tessa," she said. "Your son is filling me on the details of his sex life."

Tessa raised an eyebrow at her son and he hurried to correct Lissy.

"No . . . I meant I've done a lot more Nick sort of things. I've jet skied, and we're going to climb Mt. Stromboli. It's a volcano."

"And I think you have finally fallen in love with life," said Tessa. "It is so sad that we get to see your happiness when tragedy strikes."

Tom reached out for his mother and they stood in a close embrace for a few minutes before he pulled away.

"Can I get you a drink, Lissy?"

"A cup of tea, please."

Nick and Alex walked in together as he was pouring Lissy's tea. He looked across at his younger brother, and his stomach clenched. He felt so bloody helpless—there was nothing they could do to help, except deliver meaningless platitudes. Nick and Alex crossed the room and joined him. Nick poured a coffee and gave it to Alex, who looked at him as if he didn't know what to do with it.

"This is for Lissy." Tom handed the tea to Nick. It was time to give Nick a break—it would have been tough supporting Alex at the cemetery. He took Alex's arm and led him over to the window, searching for words, any words. But he came up with nothing.

"Don't worry, it's all been said," Alex said as if understanding his brother's search for comforting words. He put the cup on to the windowsill and coffee slopped all over the white glossy paint. "Don't try. It means nothing. Nothing will bring her back."

He stared out over the lawn and it seemed to give him comfort to speak.

"Did Nick tell you we were moving?"

Tom shook his head.

"Straight after the wedding. Only three months to go." Alex's voice shook and Tom's stomach gripped with an aching hollowness. He could not comprehend what Alex was going through. He and Emily had been together since high school.

Tom closed his eyes for a moment. At Nick and Lissy's wedding he had danced with Emily, and she had brushed her lips across his cheek and told him she was sure he would find his love in Italy. Now she would never know she'd been right.

"I got a transfer with the law firm. A big environmental job up in Brisbane." Alex's eyes filled with tears, and Tom put his arm around his brother as his voice broke.

"We've already bought a house up there and now she's gone. Bloody stoned truck driver. I could kill the bastard with my bare hands."

He let Alex vent his grief and held him close. Alex's shoulders shuddered as he drew in deep, ragged breaths.

"He's been charged. He was high on bloody uppers and went straight through the intersection. He didn't even see her coming."

Tom turned to Nick and inclined his head. Lissy came straight over with a box of tissues and Tom led Alex out to the veranda as grief consumed him.

He sat next to him, dry-eyed, staring out over the lawn focusing on all the good times they'd had in this garden when they were growing up. Life ebbed and flowed at the hands of fate. He firmed his resolve. He was not going to give up on Brianna.

Nick came out with a bottle of whisky and three glasses and crouched in front of Alex.

"It's not a permanent solution, mate, but I think a little inebriation may go a long way tonight."

He raised his eyebrows at Tom and filled three large glasses with whisky when Tom nodded his agreement. Alex picked the crystal tumbler and held it up to the late afternoon sun. A shaft of light hit the crystal and fractured into a rainbow of colours on the wall beside them.

"To my Em." He choked and drained the glass in one swallow and sat back and closed his eyes. He held his empty glass out to Nick for a refill.

Many drinks later the bottle sat empty on the table beside Tom and Nick. Alex had collapsed an hour ago and they'd carried him to his room assisted by their father. Tessa had fussed around, removed his shoes, and tucked him in like a young child. She sat on a chair next to the bed, holding Alex's hand between her own as the tears rolled down her cheeks. She looked at her other two sons and smiled sadly, motioning for them to leave.

"I'll sit with Alex for a while," she whispered.

Tom's eyes pricked and a lump formed in his throat.

Tom and Nick returned to the veranda and

Lissy was sitting waiting for them with a pizza box. Nick sat down and pulled her onto his lap and buried his face in her red gold curls.

"I don't think I could eat anything," said Tom. "Another drink will do."

"Eat," instructed Lissy.

"Yes, ma'am."

***

Tom was grateful Lissy had forced them to eat last night even though the pizza gave him indigestion. He woke up with a dry mouth and his breath smelled of whisky, but he didn't have too bad a headache, which was just as well as he had a big day ahead of him. He glanced across at the clock and did the time conversion in his head and reached for his cell phone to call Brianna and tell her he was on his way home.

Home.

He smiled.

What was the old saying? Home is where the heart is.

The call went straight to her message service and he shook his head. She'd let the battery run down again. He had more than her organisational skills to work on.

He had a quick shower, pulled on some fresh clothes, and headed downstairs. Nick and Tessa were sitting at the kitchen table chatting quietly. He made himself a quick cup of tea and sat down with them.

"Alex?" he asked.

"Still asleep," said Tessa.

"He'll have a very sore head when he wakes up," said Nick. "What are your plans today? I thought we might take him out somewhere."

Tessa placed her hand on Nick's arm and looked across at Tom. "I think it would be better if we left him alone today and didn't organise anything him. Just be here if he wants us. He needs to find his own comfort."

Tom looked across at his mother and brother. "I'm going back to Lipari tonight."

Nick appeared startled but Tessa smiled at him with a knowing look on her face.

"You can't stay here for more than two days?" asked Nick.

"No, I have something important to do."

Chapter Fifteen

Brianna looked at the missed calls displayed on the screen of her cell phone and closed her eyes. Tom had tried to call every hour for the past twelve hours before he'd given up. *At least he'll think I've let the phone die,* she thought and that gave her a small measure of comfort. The nagging feeling she'd made a big mistake tugged at her thoughts and she tried to block it. She focused on the bumping of the train wheels as they clattered rhythmically on the track. It had been cruel to leave before he came back. He'd been so upset when he left and she'd had a glimpse of the love he had for his family. But she had no choice.

Let him go. Let him go. Let him go.

Staring out the window, she looked at the mist still lingering in the valleys despite the lateness of the morning. Summer in Scotland was nothing like Lipari Island. Shivering, she pulled her wool coat around her shoulders and tucked her scarf around her bare neck. She glanced down at her hands and smiled, thinking how out of place her tanned skin looked.

She'd left the island three days ago. The

ferry to Naples, three flights, and now the final leg of her journey by train, and she was almost home. Not home to her flat in Edinburgh but home to her parents in Aviemore where she'd grown up in the snow-covered highlands of Scotland.

Ready to confront Jennifer—she couldn't think of her as Mum any more—not after the discovery she'd made in Lipari, she was trying to figure out what to say, what to ask to understand the enormity of what Jennifer and her mother Rosa had done. Her *nonno* had held her and she'd sobbed in his arms after reading the letter her mother had written before she died, and now she was going to confront Jennifer with the secret she had kept for over thirty years. No wonder she hadn't never felt love from her adopted mother. In a way she felt sorry for Jennifer. It must have been hard for her, sharing her adopted daughter with her birth mother and having to keep it a secret.

The train pulled into Kingussie station and she gathered her bags. Aviemore was next.

An hour later she pushed open the gate to her parents' retirement cottage and was pleased to see clothes flapping in the breeze. She'd been so determined to confront them, she hadn't even given thought to them being away on one of their regular trips.

Her phone rang when she was pushing open the front door. She pulled it from her pocket and sighed as she glanced down at the caller ID. She hit the off button and let Tom's call go to voicemail with a sigh, knowing she would have to talk to him sooner or later, but first she had to get her head around this mess.

"Brianna." She jumped as her father's voice boomed from the living room. "What a wonderful surprise." She slipped into his embrace and inhaled the familiar aroma of his pipe tobacco.

"Your mother's in the back garden. She'll be so happy to see you. She was only bemoaning the lack of emails from you this morning." He cupped her cheek in his large rough hands, his fingers scratchy against her skin. "Is everything okay, love? You look a wee bit unhappy."

She nodded and followed him through the back door, clenching her fists as a sharp ache lodged in her throat. These people had welcomed her to their family as a newborn baby and she should be grateful to them for the loving home they'd provided. Jennifer was on her knees weeding the vegetable patch. As much as she didn't want to hurt her parents, she needed to have it out. They owed her an explanation.

She closed her eyes and wished she were back on the island sitting on the balcony sharing a drink with Tom.

Blast you, Tom. Get out of my head. I am not going to depend on you.

Jennifer stood and pulled off her gardening gloves. It was apparent by the look on her face that she had read Brianna's expression and knew why she had come home.

"Time for a chat. We have a lot of talking to do," Brianna said.

***

An hour passed, much tea was consumed, and her parents convinced her the secrecy had been at Rosa's request.

"Love, she could see how happy you were and then she didn't want to mess with your head. All she wanted was for you to be happy and you have been, haven't you?" Jennifer put her teacup down and squeezed her daughter's hands. "We tried to persuade her, especially at the end when we knew she didn't have long, but she wouldn't have it."

"Did she tell you about the villa? Did you know she was leaving it to me?"

Jennifer shook her head. "She spoke toward the end about how if you ever married, she would leave it to you. I don't understand how you've got the villa now. She made it quite clear she wouldn't leave it to you unless you were married. She never forgave your father for leaving her as a single mother and she swore she would do as much as she could to make sure you married and settled. She wanted to provide for you, but I guess she put her own take on what happiness was. She became very bitter in the end. "

Brianna gave a short laugh and held out left hand and flashed her wedding ring. "She didn't change her mind. I got married a week after I arrived on Lipari Island."

The look on her parents' faces was priceless and Brianna gave a bitter laugh.

"And now I have to get out of it and try and keep the villa. Do we have a good lawyer?"

Her phone buzzed and she groaned, putting her head down on her arms on the table. Her voice was muffled.

"It's all too bloody complicated."

Chapter Sixteen

Tom sat alone on the balcony of Brianna's villa watching the sunrise over the sea before he started work. Silver and pink tinged the low line of clouds hovering above the horizon. It promised to be another clear and beautiful day, but he was not going to the marina. Aunt Carmen had returned from Naples and he'd promised himself he would make a start on deciphering the finances today. He couldn't believe the change in himself. A few months ago, he would have had the books balanced and computerised even if it had meant staying up all night. Now he preferred to spend his nights in Brianna's bed, and he gave little thought to his stocks and shares. They were in the hands of his broker and he trusted him to make the decisions for him.

Loneliness settled in his chest. It had sat there like a stone for the three days since he had returned to the empty villa. Luckily, Brianna had left the key for him and a brief note saying she was going back to Edinburgh and would be in touch. The disappointment had overwhelmed him, but he knew there must be a good reason for her sudden departure. Everything had been fine between them when he'd left and she had promised to stay, so something had happened. He knew he loved her and he was not going to doubt that she loved him, too. It was only a matter of time until she admitted it to herself and he had planned his strategy.

He'd reverted to list making and he hoped she appreciated it. The time had come to implement it. He pulled out his phone and checked the time. Seven a.m. here, five a.m. in Edinburgh. He knew she was not picking up his calls, because it rang out before going to her voicemail.

Time to wake up, Brianna.

He pressed send and put his phone away before pulling out the first box of papers.

Two hours later, he was sitting in the kitchen, receipts and journals spread chaotically across the table when his phone beeped.

I am.

Tom jumped to his feet and punched the air with a loud 'Yes.' Aunt Maria had arrived earlier and now she ran in from the balcony where she was watering the potted plants. "You have finished the books?" she asked.

Tom grabbed her and danced around the room. "No, but I will soon."

Aunt Maria shook her head and went back into the kitchen and Tom picked up his phone.

He typed another text

#1 I got my earring, remember?

He waited and a beep signalled the reply.

I remember.

His fingers flew over the keypad.

#2 Jet skied and didn't drown. He waited for a reply but all was quiet. He turned back to the tattered ledgers spread across the table and lasted for another two hours until the call of the boats and the fresh air won.

The phone remained silent.

***

Brianna was sitting in the office of the chief executive officer of the Burrough Medical Service waiting for her boss to finish his call. She stared out the window at the steady rain, grateful for the warmth of the air conditioning in the office. Glancing down at the phone in her hand, she closed her eyes and smiled. A picture of Tom riding a jet ski around Lipari harbour, his long black curls tangling in the breeze, his muscles flexing as he steered through the waves was implanted in her mind. And of course, the earring would be glinting in the bright sunshine.

Damn him, she thought.

"So, Brianna, you've finished the book?" her boss asked. "A lot earlier than you'd planned."

"Yes, Mick. A new me. I met someone who helped me with my time management skills." She smiled at him. "So here I am, ready to come back to work a bit earlier."

"I'd be more than happy for you to cancel your leave." Mick steepled his fingers under his chin and frowned. "But your replacement is on a six-month contract and that doesn't finish for another eight weeks. So I'm going to have to keep you on leave for at least another two months."

Brianna looked across at the window and thought for a moment. "What about in one of the other branches? Any other openings to fill in for a couple of months? I'm happy to travel."

Mick shook his head. "Things are tight at the moment. Government budget cuts, and it's getting worse by the day." He looked down at his watch. "I'm sorry, I have another appointment. So we'll expect you back in eight weeks?"

Brianna stood and her phone beeped. She ignored it and gave her full attention to her boss. "Not a problem. It was worth a try. I might even start another book."

She walked out of the office and picked up her umbrella from the circular bin at the front door.

The fates were conspiring against her.

No way was she going back to Lipari while Tom was there. She was running scared, but she knew he was going to try and convince her to make it a real marriage. It was not fair—she was only emotional because of the situation with her mother.

She was not in love with Tom. She didn't do relationships. They don't last.

Her conscience nagged. She was so confused she didn't know what she wanted.

Her phone beeped again while she was on the bus and being pigheaded she decided to ignore it. He was persistent—went with his personality type. Closing her eyes so she couldn't see the phone tempting her from the side of her bag, she tried to make a plan.

No success.

What the hell was she going to do in Edinburgh stuck in her tiny apartment for eight weeks? She was so *not* going to be tempted back to the island by some stupid text messages. The phone beeped again. She shoved it down into her bag and sighed.

He knew how she felt and if he carried on like this he was going to get hurt. Yes, he was a great friend and she loved him like a friend. He was fun to be with and they were explosive in the bedroom. But he was only a friend.

I don't do love and happy ever after. And she knew deep in her heart he would be happy with no less.

Why can't things stay the way they were?

She chewed on her lip and the phone beeped again and she pulled it angrily out of her bag.

#3 I had fun.

So did I Tomas, so did I.

#4   *Your kitchen is a mess and my clothes are on the floor. Aunt Maria won't pick them up.*

Brianna burst out laughing and typed a response.

I don't like mess.

His answer came straight back.

#5. *Got roaring drunk last week. Never again . . . been there, done that.*

The bus drew to a halt and she realised they were at her stop. She grabbed her bag and umbrella, getting to the automatic door just as it began to close.

She jumped through the door and dropped her umbrella. When she bent to pick it up her cell phone flew out of her bag and landed in a puddle.

"Shit, shit, shit. Oh, no." Distress pierced her chest and she scrabbled around in the pouring rain. The phone was sodden and she wiped it with her coat. Glancing around, the bright lights of a tearoom beckoned and she pushed open the door, grateful for the warmth inside. With shaking fingers, she slid the loose back section of the phone back into place and pressed the power button, breathing a huge sigh of relief as the phone powered on.

The waitress waited for her order while she scanned her message box.

Three new messages.

She looked up at the waitress, laughing, and

ordered a pot of tea and scones.

"Glad to see the rain hasn't upset you, lovey," the woman said.

Brianna opened her inbox.

 # 6 Didn't insult anyone on the flight back. No beautiful clinical psychologists.

Beautiful. A warm feeling stole over her and she closed her eyes. He told me I was beautiful all the time. What did he say before he left? 'You've bewitched me. You're in my blood.'

The waitress placed a steaming pot of tea and a plate of scones loaded with jam and cream in front of her. Comfort food. She looked down at the next message.

 # 7 Fall in love. Wasn't on the first list, but it happened

Oh Jesus, don't do this to me, Tom.

The phone beeped again. What the hell was the next message going to say?

Call me. Temporary staff member happy to leave now.

It was a lifeline from Mick. Disappointment surged through her. Her finger hovered over the buttons.

Chapter Seventeen

Tom pushed his bicycle through the gate of Brianna's grandfather's villa. He'd been invited up for a late lunch and was interested to find out what the old fellow wanted. The invitation had been more like a command. A brief note delivered yesterday by his driver, with a date and time in the mid-afternoon next to *'pranzo.'* Lunch. Friday, three o'clock.

Even though he'd taken a change of clothes and showered at the marina, he was hot by the time he parked his bike outside the luxurious villa. He wondered how cold it was in Scotland.

His phone had remained deathly silent since his seventh text and he had begun to worry he'd pushed her too far. Swallowing the doubt plaguing him, he rang the bell on the ornate door and waited to be summoned inside. It had been two days since his last text and it was about time he took the final step of his campaign.

"Benvenuto, figlio mio." *Signore* Caranto greeted him at the door himself.

"Still no Brianna?" the old man asked. Tom

shook his head wondered how much her grandfather knew, but he didn't answer until they were seated in the salon. *Signore* Caranto poured a large glass of red wine for each of them.

"I'm waiting for a message from her." He couldn't help himself and pulled his phone out but the screen was clear. *"Scusi."* Scrolling down to the inbox, he checked in case a message had filed itself. Nothing.

Signore Caranto looked him with sympathy. "She will come back. She love you."

Tom's head flew up.

"I see the way she look at you." The old man shook his head and leaned forward. He spoke in Italian and explained that he wanted there to be no misunderstandings, so if Tom was happy he would stay in his native language.

Tom nodded.

He listened carefully and a great sense of relief overtook him. Brianna's grandfather told him about visiting Brianna the day Tom had left for Australia. He told him about the photographs and the letter he'd given Brianna, and why she'd gone to Scotland.

The old man sat back and stared at Tom, a frown wrinkling his forehead.

"I know why you married her. And it is all right. It was her mother's wish she be married and it has all worked out good." He explained he had kept his distance until he was sure it was the right thing for his granddaughter to be here. He didn't want to be selfish. He had seen the unsettled life Rosa had lived. When he described how he'd held his granddaughter in his arms and they had made their peace, Tom closed his eyes.

He missed her so much.

It was time for the last text. He explained what he was about to do and a wide smile took years of *Signore* Carranto's lined face.

"It's time," Tom said to the old man and pulled out his phone and pressed the letters firmly and confidently.

#8 Marry me again?
#9 Love you
#10 Love you heaps
#11 Last message
#12 Over to you.

Tom put the phone on the table and picked up his wine. *Signore* Carranto sat next to him and together they watched the phone and waited. It was seconds before it buzzed and Tom grabbed it from the table. He let out a great whoop and grabbed the old man in an embrace before giving him a smacking kiss on both cheeks.

"She's on the ferry!" he exclaimed and ran for the door. "Rain check on lunch."

Grabbing his bike, he jumped on it and pedalled furiously down the hill. The afternoon breeze from the harbour cooled his cheeks as he coasted down the bumpy road, excitement zinging through his veins.

It had to be good news. It had to be yes.

She wouldn't have come home if she didn't love him.

Tom was confident and wouldn't let the niggling doubts creep in. As soon as he saw her, he'd know.

The blast of the ferry's horn announced its arrival as it turned into the harbour. The pressure wave from the bow broke the surface of the calm water. Seagulls screeched and hovered above the ferry as it drew closer to the shore. Tom put the bike outside the marina and ran down the steps to the boarding area.

Brianna stood on the top deck, her hair braided and her thick fringe blowing in the stiff afternoon breeze. She was too far away for him to see her face, but she waved wildly as soon as she saw him and he waved back.

Tom stood patiently as the ferry docked and the tourist crowd shuffled off. Leaning against the wall in the shade of the terminal building, he waited.

A high-pitched squeal ahead of him caught his attention and he stepped forward, smiling as he remembered his first sight of those long bare legs sliding to a stop at the international airport in

Sydney a few months ago. The girlish figure with a long dark braid flying behind her ran across the boardwalk in front of the ticket office and flung herself into his waiting arms. She rained kisses on his cheeks, her long legs wrapped around his hips. Tom smiled at her exuberance and dropped his head and captured her mouth with his. After a moment she pulled back and her dark gaze held his.

"I'm so happy you waited for me, Tom. I love you, love you, love you so much."

Arms looped around each other, Brianna chattered nonstop as they walked across to collect Tom's bike.

"I was wrong," she said.

"About a lot of things," said Tom.

She pretended to punch him on the arm and he stopped walking.

"I can do relationships. I just needed the right man."

"Come over here and kiss me again, woman. I missed you."

"Are you going to propose to me?"

"We're already married," he said between kisses.

"But I want to do it right."

Epilogue

As far as weddings went, well . . . it was different.

The setting was on a wild flowered-covered cliff top overlooking the azure blue sea. Mt. Stromboli put on a fine show for the guests. The bride wore a second-hand wedding dress because the groom had insisted she wore the same dress she had worn to their first wedding. The groom wore jeans and a black T-shirt, because the bride chose his outfit. The best man, Nick, held his wife's hand and their new baby gurgled as the vows were made.

The bride's grandfather held the hand of the groom's aunt. They had made their peace and the Italian cousins from the island suspected they may be attending another wedding in the not too distant future.

As the groom kissed his bride, a flurry of congratulations in Italian, and in Scottish and Australian accents surrounded them as their three families bestowed them with good wishes.

Tom had arrived holding Brianna's hand and he'd kept his arm around her for the whole ceremony. As the Italian cousins sprinkled them with confetti, he murmured against her lips.

"Have I told you what a beautiful bride you

make, Mrs. Richards?"

"Have I told you how much I love you, Mr. Richards?" Brianna lifted her head and smiled at her husband.

One man, one woman, a second wedding…for a lifetime this time.

THE END

Book 1 Nick's story: The Trouble with Paradise

Book 3 Alex's story: Outback Sunrise

Visit Annie's website to subscribe to her newsletter to stay up to date with release dates:

Other Books by Annie Seaton

Daughters of the Darling
From Across the Sea
Over the River
By the Billabong (2025)
Beneath Still Waters (2025)

A Bec Whitfield Mystery
Bowen River
Shadows on the Shore
Storm Season (2026)

Duckinwilla Days
Coming Home
Secrets and Surprises

Wishes and Whispers

Chasing Dreams

New Beginnings

Home to the Outback
Lucy
Angie
Jemima
Isabella

Porter Sisters Series

ANNIE SEATON

Kakadu Sunset
Daintree
Diamond Sky
Hidden Valley
Larapinta
Kakadu Dawn

Others
Whitsunday Dawn
Undara
Osprey Reef
East of Alice
One Summer in Tuscany
Four Seasons Short and Sweet
Follow the Sun
Ten Days in Paradise
Deadly Secrets
Adventures in Time
Silver Valley Witch
The Emerald Necklace
A Clever Christmas
Christmas with the Boss
Her Christmas Star
The Emerald Necklace

The Augathella Girls Series
Outback Roads
Outback Sky
Outback Escape
Outback Wind
Outback Dawn
Outback Moonlight
Outback Dust

Beach House
Beach Music
Beach Walk
Beach Dreams
The House on the Hill Boxed Set

Second Chance Bay Series
Her Outback Playboy
Her Outback Protector
Her Outback Haven
Her Outback Paradise
Boxed Set
The McDougalls of Second Chance Bay Boxed Set

Love Across Time Series
Come Back to Me
Follow Me
Finding Home
The Threads that Bind
Boxed Set
Love Across Time 1-4

Bindarra Creek
Worth the Wait
Full Circle
Secrets of River Cottage
A Clever Christmas
A Place to Belong
Hearts in Harmony

Awards

2024: Finalist – Romantic suspense category, RUBY award for *From Across the Sea.*

2023: Winner - Long contemporary novel category, RUBY award for *Larapinta.*

2023: Finalist - Australian Romance Readers Awards for *Kakadu Dawn,* the sixth and final book in the Porter Sisters series.

2018 and 2020: Finalist - for the NZ KORU Award.

2017: Winner - Best Established Author of the Year 2017 AUSROM

2017: Winner - Author of the Year 2014 AUSROM
Best Established Author, Ausrom Readers' Choice.

2016, 2017, 2018, 2019: Longlisted - Sisters in Crime Davitt Awards

2016: Finalist - Book of the Year, Long Romance, RWA Ruby Awards for *Kakadu Sunset*

2015: Winner - Best Established Author of the Year AUSROM

About the Author

Annie lives in Australia, on the beautiful north coast of New South Wales. She sits in her writing chair and looks out over the tranquil Pacific Ocean.
She writes contemporary romance and loves telling the stories that always have a happily ever after. She lives with her very own hero of many years and they share their home with Barney, the rag doll kitten, who hides when the four grandchildren come to visit.
Stay up to date with her latest releases at her website: http://www.annieseaton.net

If you would like to stay up to date with Annie's releases, subscribe to her newsletter here: http://www.annieseaton.net